Alice

ALICE IN LACE

Books by Phyllis Reynolds Naylor

SHILOH BOOKS
Shiloh
Shiloh Season
Saving Shiloh

THE ALICE BOOKS
Starting with Alice
Alice in Blunderland
Lovingly Alice
The Agony of Alice
Alice in Rapture, Sort of
Reluctantly Alice
All but Alice
Alice in April
Alice In-Between
Alice the Brave
Alice in Lace
Outrageously Alice
Achingly Alice
Alice on the Outside
The Grooming of Alice
Alice Alone
Simply Alice
Patiently Alice
Including Alice
Alice on Her Way
Alice in the Know
Dangerously Alice

THE BERNIE MAGRUDER BOOKS
*Bernie Magruder and the
  Case of the Big Stink*
*Bernie Magruder and the
  Disappearing Bodies*
*Bernie Magruder and the
  Haunted Hotel*
*Bernie Magruder and the
  Drive-thru Funeral Parlor*
*Bernie Magruder and the
  Bus Station Blowup*
*Bernie Magruder and the
  Pirate's Treasure*
*Bernie Magruder and the
  Parachute Peril*
*Bernie Magruder and the
  Bats in the Belfry*

THE CAT PACK BOOKS
The Grand Escape
The Healing of Texas Jake
Carlotta's Kittens
Polo's Mother

THE YORK TRILOGY
Shadows on the Wall
Faces in the Water
Footprints at the Window

THE WITCH BOOKS
Witch's Sister
Witch Water
The Witch Herself
The Witch's Eye
Witch Weed
The Witch Returns

PICTURE BOOKS
King of the Playground
The Boy with the Helium Head
Old Sadie and the
  Christmas Bear
Keeping a Christmas Secret
Ducks Disappearing
I Can't Take You Anywhere
Sweet Strawberries
Please DO Feed the Bears
Books for Young Readers
Josie's Troubles
How Lazy Can You Get?
All Because I'm Older
Maudie in the Middle
One of the Third-Grade
  Thonkers
Roxie and the Hooligans

BOOKS FOR MIDDLE READERS
Walking Through the Dark
How I Came to Be a Writer
Eddie, Incorporated
The Solomon System
The Keeper
Beetles, Lightly Toasted
The Fear Place
Being Danny's Dog
Danny's Desert Rats
Walker's Crossing

BOOKS FOR OLDER READERS
A String of Chances
Night Cry
The Dark of the Tunnel
The Year of the Gopher
Send No Blessings
Ice
Sang Spell
Jade Green
Blizzard's Wake

ALICE IN LACE

PHYLLIS REYNOLDS NAYLOR

ALADDIN MIX

NEW YORK LONDON TORONTO SYDNEY

ALADDIN MIX
Simon & Schuster Children's Publishing Division
1230 Avenue of the Americas, New York, NY 10020
Copyright © 1996 by Phyllis Reynolds Naylor
All rights reserved, including the right of reproduction in whole or in part in any form.
ALADDIN PAPERBACKS and related logo and ALADDIN MIX and related logo
are registered trademarks of Simon & Schuster, Inc.
Also available in an Atheneum Books for Young Readers hardcover edition.
Manufactured in the United States of America
First Aladdin MIX edition February 2009
2 4 6 8 10 9 7 5 3 1
The Library of Congress has cataloged the hardcover edition as follows:
Naylor, Phyllis Reynolds.
Alice in lace / Phyllis Reynolds Naylor.—1st ed.
p. cm.
"A Jean Karl book."
Summary: While planning a wedding as part of an assignment for her
eighth-grade health class, Alice thinks about her father's and older brother's love lives
and learns that you cannot prepare for all of life's decisions.
ISBN-13: 978-0-689-80358-1 (hc)
ISBN-10: 0-689-80358-3 (hc)
[1. Schools—Fiction. 2. Decision making—Fiction. 3. Single-parent family—Fiction.
4. Family life—Fiction.] I. Title.
PZ7.N24Akf 1996
[Fic]—dc20
95-30903
ISBN-13: 978-1-4169-7543-4 (MIX pbk)
ISBN-10: 1-4169-7543-8 (MIX pbk)

To Jaime Hinton, with love

Contents

$\mathscr{T}$HINKING AHEAD

$\mathscr{P}$atrick and I were getting married, Pamela was pregnant, and Elizabeth was buying a car.

It all happened in our health class, in a unit called Critical Choices. We had entered eighth grade fresh from a summer in Mark Stedmeister's swimming pool, and one week later we were saddled with all the cares of adulthood.

"What we're going to study," Mr. Everett said, "is how the choices you make now can affect the rest of your life."

He was new to our school this year. Mr. Everett was probably about thirty and really tall, maybe six foot five, wore Dockers, and rolled his shirtsleeves up above his elbows. When he talked, he leaned against the blackboard, arms folded over his chest, feet crossed at the ankles, a lock of blond hair hanging over one eye. A younger version of Robert Redford, Pamela described him.

His smile was what got to us. It was warm. Friendly. You couldn't call it flirtatious. He just gave the impression of really loving his job.

"When you come to class tomorrow," he told us, "you'll each receive a hypothetical situation in which you will find yourself for the next five weeks. Your assignment is to get as much information as you can about your particular problem."

"Like . . . what kind of problems?" Mark Stedmeister asked.

The Redford smile again: "Everything from totaling the car to having a baby."

"*Moi*—a baby?" Mark said, looking shocked, and everyone laughed.

"You'll find out tomorrow," said Mr. Everett. "Now listen up. Your grade will depend not necessarily on how you deal with your problem, but on the larger view you take. I'll want to know how your solution affects you, the people around you, society, the works."

Mr. Everett thinks big.

Leave it to Elizabeth to worry, however.

"I'll just die if he makes me pregnant," she said as we left class.

"Watch how you say that," Pamela joked.

But Elizabeth worried that if she got the assignment for teenage pregnancy, she might have to go to the doctor for her first pelvic exam just so she could write it up for her report. She's hopeless.

That night at the dinner table, I told Dad and Lester, my soon-to-be twenty-one-year-old brother, about Mr. Everett's class and how I was going to learn to make decisions.

"Excellent idea!" said Dad. "For once the schools are teaching something practical."

2

"I'm going to learn what to do if I total the car or get pregnant," I added.

Dad stopped chewing.

"Will they accept questions from the outside?" asked Lester. "Will they help me decide between a brunette and a redhead?"

But Dad interrupted. "Al," he said, "if you're thinking, even remotely, of having sex . . ."

"I'm not," I told him. "Well, I *think* about it, of course, but I'm not about to do anything."

My real name is Alice McKinley, but Dad and Lester call me Al. I think it's because Mom died when I was small that Dad freaks out about me sometimes. It's true that he and Lester don't know diddly about raising a girl, but it bothers Dad a lot more than it bothers Lester.

I chewed thoughtfully on a carrot stick. "Actually, the situations he's going to assign us seem sort of hokey. Who sits down and thinks, 'I guess I'll go total the car tonight' or 'Dad, I want to have a teenage pregnancy'? Sometimes things just happen."

"That's the point," Dad said. "These things happen because nobody thought they would. Nobody did any planning. Somebody has a few beers and gets in his car, or a girl has sex with her boyfriend. They're not thinking 'car wreck.' They're not thinking 'baby.'"

I sighed. Life, as far as I could see, was going to be a sort of obstacle course, with detours, yield signs, stop signs, and cautions.

"What I wish," I said, "is that I was born with a built-in buzzer, and whenever I was about to do something incredibly stupid, it beeped."

"You were," said Dad. "It's called conscience."

"Dad, every time I listen to my conscience it sounds just like you."

"Imagine that," he said.

When we got to health class the next day, Mr. Everett went down the rows passing out worksheets. Each worksheet was different, with one of our names at the top, and as people read their assignments, they groaned or whooped or giggled.

Behind me, Elizabeth gave a gigantic sigh of relief. "All I have to do is buy a car!" she said. "Holy Mary, thank you, thank you, thank you!"

Patrick and I got the same situation. We were engaged to be married, our assignments read, and for the next five weeks we were to plan the wedding and honeymoon, rent an apartment, buy furniture, and work out a budget. I could feel my face redden, but secretly I was pleased. I've known Patrick Long since sixth grade, and he's been my boyfriend on and off. At the moment we were on again. Mr. Everett must have noticed.

"Hey, Patrick! Way to go!" Mark called out. All over the room kids were teasing us.

Patrick looks a lot like Mr. Everett, actually, only younger.

He has red hair and he plays the drums. His dad is a diplomat or something, and they've lived in a lot of different countries. I guess it wasn't as exciting for him to marry a girl who was born in Chicago as it was for me to marry him, but he was smiling at me.

"Mr. Everett," called Brian, who is probably *the* most handsome guy in eighth grade. "If Alice and Patrick are getting married, does this entitle them to all the . . . uh . . . privileges of married life?"

More laughter.

"*Hypothetical* situation, Brian," said Mr. Everett.

"Hypo- what?"

"Look it up."

Brian's situation was a DWI offense, Jill had to arrange a funeral for her grandmother, Karen got arrested for shoplifting, Mark had supposedly gotten a girl pregnant, Pamela *was* pregnant, and Elizabeth was buying a car. And this was just the crowd I hang out with. Some of the others had it worse.

Now all the attention focused on Pamela.

"What am I supposed to do, Mr. Everett?" she asked. "If I'm already pregnant, what's there to decide?"

"What's there to *decide*?" The teacher gave her a quizzical look. "You're going to be a *mother, Pamela.*"

The whole class broke into laughter. When it died down, he went on: "You're going to have another person to look out for, you have to live somewhere, you have to support

5

the two of you—and you ask me what there is to decide?"

Pamela shrugged. "Well . . . I mean . . . what if I choose an abortion?"

"What if you *do*? That's what we want to know. What would that mean to you? Or what happens if you decide to give the baby up for adoption? There are 'what ifs' all over the place. That's what this class is about. Thinking things through *before* they happen. *Planning* your life instead of letting events decide things for you."

"Aren't we really supposed to figure out what *you* think we should do?" asked Karen.

"If I'm a good teacher, you won't even know what I think," Mr. Everett told her. "All the thinking's got to be done by you. And maybe there isn't just one good solution, but several. Have you considered that?"

I'd wondered if there would be enough stuff in this assignment to fill up the next five weeks, and now I knew there was enough to think about for the next five *years*.

What was embarrassing, though, was that Pamela was supposed to be pregnant, and Mark was supposed to have gotten a girl pregnant, though not necessarily Pamela, but Mark and Pamela weren't speaking, having broken up just before school started. Pamela was going with Brian now, so Mark and Brian weren't speaking, either.

Worse yet, Elizabeth had only been going with Tom Perona for one week when she found out he had *two* ID bracelets, and had given one to a girl at St. John's, where he goes to school. Pamela and I were furious with Tom. It couldn't have happened at a worse time. Elizabeth had *finally* gotten to the place where she could kiss comfortably, and now she had to find out that Tom was two-timing her again, just as he did the summer after sixth grade.

"He's nothing but a Tom-cat, Elizabeth. Forget him," I said.

But Elizabeth blamed us instead. She said her breath must smell or her body smelled, and we hadn't told her. If a boy had been going with her only a week before he started seeing someone else, there obviously was something wrong with her, and that's what came of getting physically close to boys. She simply wasn't ready yet. I sort of agreed, knowing Elizabeth.

"You should date a guy from our own school," Pamela said. "If Tom's around other girls all day and never sees you, he's bound to be attracted to somebody else."

But all Elizabeth would say was, "If *you* had bad breath or something, I'd tell *you*," so we just gave up.

"Hey, Alice," Patrick said, coming up behind me after class and tickling the back of my neck. "We've got to do this assignment together. We're engaged, right?" He gave my waist a little squeeze. "What do you want to do first?"

We stopped there in the hall and looked over Mr. Everett's assignment:

> Assume that you are high school graduates with no college training, and the maximum you have to spend on your wedding, honeymoon, apartment, and furniture is $5,000.

"Five thousand dollars!" I gasped. "We're rich, Patrick!"

"Hardly," he said.

"I'll call the *Post* and find out how much it costs to announce the engagement," I told him.

"I'll ask a travel agent about a honeymoon in Hawaii," said Patrick.

"Hawaii?" I said. "I don't want to go to Hawaii."

"You don't? Where do you want to go?"

I hadn't even thought about it, really. I just wanted a choice in the matter. I tried to think of all the places I'd ever wanted to visit. "Well, Disney World, maybe."

"*Disney* World? You want to go to Disney World on your *honey*moon?"

"Well . . . I want to have a *say* in it, Patrick. You can't just write down that we're going to Hawaii without asking me first."

"Good grief, they've only been engaged for ten minutes and they're quarreling already," Pamela teased.

"Okay," said Patrick. "Let's each make a list of the five places we'd most like to go on a honeymoon and see if we can agree on one of them."

That evening I explained our assignment to Dad. "Where did you and Mom go on your honeymoon?" I asked.

"To tell the truth, Al, we got married when I was in graduate school, and I was finishing up my thesis. We didn't have either the time or the money, so we just went camping in a state park for the weekend—slept in a tent out under the stars."

I stared. "You didn't have a honeymoon?"

"We didn't *want* a honeymoon right then. We wanted for me to finish my thesis and get a job, and we took a trip a year later when there was time to enjoy it."

I went out on the porch where Lester was reading one of his philosophy books on the swing, and sat down beside him. He groaned automatically as he always does when I get near him, warding me off. So I didn't say anything, just pulled one knee up on the swing and turned sideways so I could watch his face while the swing moved back and forth.

Lester has a black mustache and there was a little hair on one end of it that was bent into a loop, as though the other end were growing back into his face again.

I slowly reached out and gave a little tug to see if I could get the end loose.

"Al, what the heck!" said Lester, slapping at my hand.

"I just wanted to see if you had an ingrown hair on your mustache," I whispered. "Go ahead and study, Les. Don't mind me."

Lester turned a page and went on reading.

I pushed the swing slowly with one foot and studied my brother. I was trying to decide whether, if I were a twenty-year-old woman, I'd think he was cute.

I do like his mustache. He has nice hair, too, even though it's a little thin on top. He's taller than Dad, not skinny, but not plump either. I wondered if he kept his nails manicured. He had his fingers curled under the edge of his book, though, and I had to bend over to see them.

Lester put down the book. "Al, do you want something?"

"Am I bothering you, Lester?"

"What do you think?"

"Well, I just have one quick question."

"*How* quick?"

"You can probably answer in one word."

"The answer is no," said Lester. "Whatever the question, the answer is no."

I plopped back against the swing and sulked.

"Okay, Al," he sighed. "One question. What do you want?"

I told him about the assignment Patrick and I had to do for our Critical Choices unit, and how we couldn't agree on where to go for the honeymoon. I wanted Lester to think of someplace far away and exotic that I could suggest to Patrick.

"Istanbul," said Lester, picking up his book again. "Now beat it."

I went back in the house and wrote it down on a piece of paper. Then I got out our *World Atlas* to choose four more places, and wrote them down under Istanbul: Fairbanks, Leipzig, Sydney, and the Amazon.

I called Patrick. "Istanbul," I said.

"What?"

"That's where I want to go on our honeymoon."

"Really?" said Patrick, sounding surprised.

"Yes, I've always wanted to see Istanbul," I said.

"Good," said Patrick.

I had barely hung up when the phone rang. It was Aunt Sally, from Chicago. She calls us every week or so to make sure that Dad hasn't remarried without telling her, that Lester hasn't been in a car wreck, and that I'm eating all my vegetables.

"How are things?" she asked.

"We're doing all right," I told her. "Busy as usual."

"Anything exciting happening there in Maryland?" she asked, as she always does when she doesn't get enough information out of her first question.

"Well," I said, "Elizabeth's buying a car, Patrick and I are getting married, and Pamela's pregnant."

I don't know why I do that to Mom's older sister. There was a silence so long I was afraid she might have had a heart attack.

"Put your father on the line," she said hoarsely.

"Joke! Joke!" I cried. "It's an assignment we have to do for health class. We have to make all these decisions about what we'd do if we were in certain situations."

"I can't believe this!" said Aunt Sally. "Has your teacher lost her mind?"

"It's a man," I told her.

"I don't see any good coming out of this at all, Alice.

Talking about things like this will just make students want to try them."

Why do adults think that way, I wonder? Why do they think that if we hear or read about something, we'll rush right out and do it? Even suicide. When Denise Whitlock stepped in front of a train last spring, the principal put the whole school on suicide alert. As though we would all rush down to Amtrak like lemmings and stand in front of the first train to leave Union Station.

"He's a good teacher," I said, and added, "He looks like Robert Redford."

Aunt Sally gave a deep sigh. "I didn't think I could survive Carol's junior high and high school years, and now I've got to worry about yours."

"Doesn't it help to know that Lester is looking out for me?" I asked.

"I'll only get to the cardiac unit that much sooner," said Aunt Sally.

"Al," Dad called to me about nine. "When's your next dental appointment?"

I wandered into the dining room where Dad had our calendar there on the table—our *new* table with eight chairs. I figured our house was beginning to look more and more like the kind of house we'd had when Mom was alive.

"I don't know," I told him. "It's the last thing on my mind."

Dad gave me an exasperated look. He'd been having a pretty short fuse lately. "Well, when were you there last?"

I shrugged. "I don't *know*."

He flipped through the pages. "Can you remember the *month*, Al? Wouldn't it be here on the calendar?"

"If it is, *I* didn't put it there."

"Then how on earth do you know when it's time for another checkup?" he said, tossing his pencil down. "Don't you *plan* anything?"

Were Dad and Mr. Everett in cahoots, I wondered, or is this what happens when you get older—your brain divides your life into little two-inch squares where you write down your plans for each day?

I leaned over the calendar and looked back through the pages to see if anything would help me remember. I was surprised to see all the little notes that had been written in those squares. Even *Lester* had put stuff down. The only dates I remember are when I'm going to the movies with Patrick, when assignments are due, and when I can expect my next period. Beyond that, I haven't a clue as to what's going to happen to me.

"*Think*," said Dad. "We got a card from the dentist saying you haven't been there for two years. That can't be possible, can it?"

"I suppose it could," I said. "I guess I only remember being there the summer after we moved from Takoma Park."

"Good grief," said Dad. "Al, you are now in charge of putting all appointments on this calendar. You are to call the dentist, make an appointment, and ask the nurse to send you a card every six months to remind you."

"I have been getting cards," I said. "I just . . . didn't do anything about them."

He stared at me incredulously. "Do you want your teeth to rot? Do you want to sit around beating your gums together when you're forty, and live on a diet of stewed meat? For heaven's sake, Al, take charge of your life here."

I figured Dad was upset because he knew if Aunt Sally ever found out, she'd . . .

"And don't tell your Aunt Sally," he bellowed as he left the room.

$\mathscr{S}$PEAKING OF LUST

$\mathscr{I}$t *was* fun to be in eighth grade. The younger kids looked so green, so uptight. In some ways, I guess, we were beginning to feel a little more relaxed about our bodies—Elizabeth, Pamela, and I.

In eighth grade, I noticed, guys and girls usually ate at the same tables—a lot of us, anyway. We'd steal food off each other's trays, lean against each other when we laughed, walk down the halls with our arms around each other—sometimes there would be six of us abreast. We weren't as self-conscious about things, and it felt good.

In other ways, though, we weren't relaxed about bodies at all. Elizabeth's mother was going on her ninth month of pregnancy, and she was absolutely huge. It looked as though she were carrying a volleyball in her abdomen. She sort of waddled for balance, and when she sat down, it was on the edge of her chair so that her stomach could hang out into space. I know that all three of us—Elizabeth, Pamela, and I—were wondering how it would feel to give birth to a volleyball.

"Everything stretches, Al," Dad told me once when I said that the idea of having a baby frightened me. "It's not as though a baby comes ripping and tearing out of you."

"Whatever," I told him. I was beginning to sound like Elizabeth. I didn't even want to think about it.

I didn't imagine I would ever feel as comfortable about my body as Marilyn Rawley is about hers. She's Lester's girl-friend. Current girlfriend. Well, *one* of Lester's girlfriends. I never actually know who he's dating until a girl calls on the phone or shows up at the house.

Lester's birthday was the second week of September, and Marilyn's present to him, he told me, would be the dinner of his choice, cooked and served by Marilyn in the costume of his choice. I asked Lester what he chose, and he said surf and turf, served by Marilyn in knee-high boots and leopard-skin bikini.

"Dad," I said that evening, "what are we going to do for Lester's twenty-first birthday?"

Dad was sitting at the piano, going over some sheet music. He's manager of the Melody Inn, a music store in Silver Spring, Maryland, and every so often he brings music home to try out.

"I'm not sure. He's pretty much got the weekend sewed up, from what I understand," Dad said. "He's going out celebrating with some of his friends Friday night, and Marilyn is cooking for him on Saturday. I was thinking of telling him to come down to the store and choose a few CDs."

My problem was that I had spent almost all my money on clothes. I couldn't believe how much taller I was this September than last. None of my jeans fit right anymore. I couldn't think of a thing to buy Lester for $1.87, which was all I had left.

Then I got an idea. I figured that if Marilyn Rawley was giving him a home-cooked meal served by an attractive woman, namely herself, it was probably the present he wanted most. She should know. Why didn't I serve him breakfast? Me serving breakfast in a bathing suit was no big deal, of course, but what if Elizabeth and Pamela both helped? Breakfast in bed, served by *three* girls in bikinis? Since Pamela and Elizabeth have both had crushes on my brother for a couple of years now, I figured they'd jump at the chance.

Pamela did. "Can I wear anything I want, Alice?" she asked.

"As long as it's decent," I told her. Knowing Pamela, you have to cut her off at the pass.

"I'll wear the cat costume I wore in my tap recital," she said.

I thought Elizabeth would be happy to help out, too, but she surprised me.

"That is so *sexist,* Alice! A woman dressing up as a man's fantasy and *serving* him! Why doesn't she just sign on as his slave or something?"

"Well, if you don't want to do it, that's okay," I told her.

17

"Maybe Lester cooks for Marilyn on *her* birthday, I don't know."

"I'll come over and help you make breakfast for him, but I won't wear a bikini," she said.

The more I thought about it, the more I wondered if maybe Elizabeth wasn't right, and we were just going along with the idea of women as sex objects. So that night, when Lester and I were making dinner, I said, "Do you ever think of me as a sex object, Lester? I want the truth."

"Are you crazy?"

"I really want to know."

"You're my *sister,* Al."

"So? I mean in your *fantasies,* Lester. I want the absolute truth: Have you ever dreamed about me?"

Lester was still gaping.

"Well, *have* you?" I asked.

He blinked, and went back to layering the cheese on the noodles, while I added spoonfuls of tomato sauce.

"As a matter of fact," he said, "I dreamed about you just the other night."

I leaned over and stared up into his face. "Really? Can you tell me what it was? I mean, even if it's embarrassing, Lester, I'll understand."

"You don't want to hear it."

"I *do,* Les! Please! I won't be mad or anything. Was I a sex object?"

"Well, you were naked."

"I was? Go on, Les. We can't help what we dream, you know. I just want to understand how a man's mind works, that's all."

"Okay. Are you ready for this now?"

I nodded.

"You were walking down the street naked as a jaybird and all the dogs were barking."

I waited.

"And . . .?"

"That's it."

My face fell. "That's all of the dream? The dogs were barking?"

"Yep."

"But what were you thinking? What were you *feeling* in the dream?"

"I was thinking about calling 911 and having you arrested."

I should have been talking to God instead of Lester, I decided. I should have been asking him why he put brothers on this earth in the first place.

"Okay, question number two," I told him. "If I ever asked you to cook dinner for me in your swim trunks, would you?"

"Not a chance," said Lester.

Maybe I hadn't asked it right. "If *Marilyn* asked you to make dinner for her in your swim trunks, would you?"

"Of course," said Lester.

It was all a matter of priorities.

On Saturday, Dad left early for the Melody Inn. Lester works part-time at Maytag, and had to be there by ten, so I figured Pamela, Elizabeth, and I would go in his room just before his alarm clock went off. Pamela came over, just as she said, in her cat costume. I'd forgotten exactly what it looks like, but it certainly wasn't a Halloween costume. If the Playboy Club featured cats instead of bunnies, that's what Pamela looked like. The short little cat suit was skintight over her body, with black net stockings.

I had on my bathing suit, but the air was chilly, so I wore Lester's University of Maryland sweatshirt over the top. Elizabeth arrived wearing a long Laura Ashley dress with a high neck, in protest, she said, of Lester's fantasies.

"Is he up yet?" Pamela asked.

"No. He was out with the guys last night, so I know he's tired."

We made all his favorites. Freshly squeezed orange juice was Elizabeth's job. French toast was Pamela's. I made the bacon and coffee, and we set it all on a tray with a little card. *Happy Birthday, Les, from your loving sister and her friends,* it said.

At twenty-four past eight, we went upstairs. I went first to open his door, Elizabeth carried the coffee pot, and Pamela had the tray.

I tapped on Lester's door. "Les?"

No answer. I waited, then tapped again, and finally poked

my head inside. Lester was sound asleep and snoring. He was lying on his side, one arm up over his face, his mouth wide open.

I looked over at Elizabeth and Pamela and nodded.

"Happy birthday to you," we sang, or rather, *they* sang, since I'm the McKinley who's tone deaf, but I mouthed the words.

"Happy birthday to you, happy birthday, dear Lester . . ."

Lester pulled his arm away from his face, and one eye opened. I was directly in his line of vision, and could see him staring at me in my bathing suit and his sweatshirt.

Then he must have realized that the music was coming from someone else, not me, and lifted his head off his pillow. He blinked and stared at Pamela in her cat suit, then at Elizabeth, and dived back under the sheet.

". . . happy birthday to you!" they finished.

"Al, if you want to live, get them out of here," came a voice from under the covers.

"Don't you know what day this is?" I asked. "It's your birthday!"

"It's a nightmare," said Lester.

I couldn't hide my disappointment as Pamela set the tray down on his dresser. "It's your present from me, Lester! We fixed everything you like for breakfast, so you could eat it in bed."

There was a long, low sigh from under the sheet. "Al, you want to give me a present?"

"Yes! *This* is your—"

"Thank you very much. Now will you take your friends downstairs and promise not to come up again?"

"All right," I said. I was getting the message, and realized it had been a dumb idea. "I just, well, since Marilyn's going to cook for you in her bathing suit, I—"

"Who said anything about a bathing suit?" said the voice under the covers.

"You said . . . a bikini. . . ."

I stared at Elizabeth and Pamela. Pamela giggled, but Elizabeth was in shock.

We left the tray in Lester's room and went back down to the kitchen. We sat around the table and stared at each other.

"That is plainly immoral," said Elizabeth.

Since my family's not too big on sin, I wasn't all that sure. But then Pamela got into the act.

"What's immoral, Elizabeth?"

"A man asking a woman to go topless and they're not even married."

"There's nothing wrong with topless," said Pamela. And then we remembered that her parents are nudists. They go bottomless as well.

"Well, in *my* family, it is," said Elizabeth.

Now I was really confused. "Are certain things sins in one family and not another?" I asked.

"It's in the Bible," said Elizabeth.

"Where?" Pamela challenged. "Give me the exact verse, Elizabeth, where it says it's a sin to go topless."

I was beginning to feel this really *was* a nightmare. I was sitting here in my bathing suit and sweatshirt listening to an oversized cat talking religion with a girl in a granny gown, and I was supposed to be at my Saturday morning job at the Melody Inn in twenty-five minutes.

"Well, the Bible talks about lust," Elizabeth told her. "It's the same thing."

"But how do you know Lester is lusting after Marilyn? All you know is that she's going to cook dinner in her underwear," Pamela said.

Elizabeth was sitting with her hands folded on the table, eyes down, and suddenly she said, "You're right. I don't have any business criticizing Lester and Marilyn, and I'm sorry I said anything."

Pamela and I both stared. This was Elizabeth talking? *Saint* Elizabeth? The same girl who had gone to confession only a few weeks ago because she'd read some of the racier parts of *Tales from the Arabian Nights* aloud?

As we stared, I saw the color creeping up her neck until her whole face looked flushed.

"The . . . truth is . . .," she said, still looking down at the table, "I'm in love."

Now we *were* staring. Our mouths hung open, in fact. Had she and Tom Perona made up again? She was actually talking *love*?

"Well . . . that's great, Elizabeth!" I said. "Has he asked you to go with him? Steady, I mean?"

"Of course not!" Elizabeth said. "He's married!"

23

"What?"

And then we saw tears in her eyes. "It's Mr. Everett," she said. "I can't help it. I'm in love with him."

I slapped the side of my head to see if I was dreaming. I should have been slapping Elizabeth to knock some sense into her.

"Elizabeth, listen! You've got a bad case of puppy love, believe me!" Pamela told her.

"I don't care what it is. It's love and it hurts," Elizabeth went on, and I began to believe her. "I think about him before I go to sleep at night. He's the first thing on my mind in the morning. I try to imagine what he's doing every minute. I even. . ." Now her cheeks were *really* red, ". . . imagine how he looks in the . . . the shower."

We sat in stunned silence. Only last summer one of us, Pamela, had had her breast touched by a stranger, and now one of us was in love with a married man. *Elizabeth,* of all people!

Suddenly I wanted to be a seventh grader again. I wanted the protection of being a shapeless, self-conscious girl who didn't have to worry about what I'd wear if I ever cooked surf and turf for my boyfriend.

"Don't do anything rash, Elizabeth," I heard Pamela saying. "I mean, don't try to take him away from his wife and children."

"I wouldn't try anything like that!" said Elizabeth. "What do you think I am? All I want is for him to notice me. Just to smile and talk to me and make me feel special. He doesn't even have to touch me. I just want to know he understands and cares."

I was beginning to wonder if they shouldn't lock up the three of us for the duration of eighth grade, when I heard footsteps in the hallway. Lester walked into the kitchen in his Mickey Mouse shorts, bringing back the tray.

"Yikes!" he said. "You're still here! The granny, the cat-lady, and the girl in my sweatshirt. Don't mind the shorts, ladies."

Pamela laughed and turned away, but Elizabeth frankly stared, and Lester scooted out of the kitchen again as fast as he could.

"Well, there's another first for you, Elizabeth," I said. "You've seen my brother in his Mickey Mouse shorts and you're in love with a married man. If this is what eighth grade is like, I can't wait till we get to ninth."

$\mathscr{T}$HE COURSE OF TRUE LOVE

"$\mathscr{I}$ don't think we can afford Istanbul."

Patrick and I sat on the couch in the living room that afternoon with our notebooks scattered around the coffee table. I'd just got back from my job at the Melody Inn, where I work three hours on Saturdays doing whatever Dad says to do, and I was trying to eat a salami sandwich while Patrick went over our finances.

It was hard to find a time we were both free, because Patrick is in band at school, and he's also on the school newspaper and the debate team. He had wanted to go out for the swim team, but it interfered with track, and Patrick's really good at track.

Usually I'm not allowed to have boys in when I'm home alone, but we needed a place to work, and besides, I was eating lunch. I figure not much can happen to a girl while she's eating lunch.

"Why can't we afford Istanbul?" I asked. "We've got five thousand dollars, according to Mr. Everett."

"Mom says she thinks we should use half of it for the

wedding, and the rest for the honeymoon, our first month's rent, and some furniture," Patrick told me.

"How much would it cost to go to Istanbul?"

"Couple thousand apiece, probably."

"Scratch Istanbul," I said.

"What we need to do is make a list of everything we'd need to get married, figure out the cost, and see what we have left over for a honeymoon, rent, and furniture. What kind of a wedding do you want?" Patrick asked me.

I didn't even know what kind of a party I wanted when I reached sixteen.

"The usual, I suppose," I said.

"Let's start with the engagement announcement in the *Washington Post.*"

"I checked that already. It's one hundred twenty-five dollars for ten lines, three hundred twenty-five dollars for ten lines and a photo."

"So, let's go with just ten lines," said Patrick, and wrote it down in his notebook. "What else do you want?"

"Well, invitations, cake, photographer—isn't that about it?"

"We're hardly getting started," Patrick said. "What about the band for the reception? The music at the wedding? The minister? The organist?"

"We have to pay the minister?" I gasped.

"Of course! Then we've got flowers, food, renting a hall, wine, tuxedos . . ."

"My dress . . ."

27

"The limo—and that's just the wedding," said Patrick. "After that you've got the plane tickets to wherever we're going, the hotel, food, entertainment."

"What about a ring?" I said in this incredibly small voice.

"Oh, yeah, I forgot. I could easily spend a thousand on that."

No way, I thought, would I ever wear a ring worth a thousand dollars. What if I lost it? What if it fell down the toilet? Maybe I didn't need a diamond at all.

"Just a simple gold band would be fine," I told him.

We settled on a thin gold band for $65. Then we looked up wedding dresses in a J. C. Penney catalog. The cheapest one I could find was $275. I hated it, but then, what could I do? Not only was Istanbul no longer a possibility, but neither was Hawaii. And a reception for two hundred people with live music was out.

Dad had taken the afternoon off from work and driven Miss Summers up to the Catoctin Mountains to pick apples. Miss Summers teaches English at our school, and had started going out with Dad last December. I was sort of hoping he'd have her with him when he came back, because he hadn't seen her for a while, but when he walked in four hours later, he was alone. They obviously had picked some apples, though, because Dad was eating one.

"Where's Sylvia?" I asked. When I'm around her, I call her Miss Summers, but I wanted to impress Patrick.

"I dropped her off at home with a half bushel of winesaps.

She wants to make applesauce," Dad said. He ambled on over to the coffee table. "Homework?"

"We're planning our wedding," I said and saw Dad blanch for a moment before he remembered.

"How much is it going to cost me?" he joked. "As father of the bride, do I have anything to say about this?"

"We've got to cover everything for five thousand dollars—wedding, honeymoon, rent, and furniture," I told him.

Dad gave a low whistle. "Well, I suppose I can come up with that much for my favorite daughter."

He took another bite of apple, then went out on the porch. I could hear the slow creak of the swing. Maybe he was thinking that it wouldn't be long before his favorite daughter was planning her *real* wedding.

"Okay," Patrick said and dug his hand into the sack of chips I'd put on the coffee table. "Two hundred seventy-five dollars for a dress, sixty-five for a ring, one hundred twenty-five for the engagement announcement. About music, now, I want a live band—I don't want any disc jockey playing records and making dumb remarks. I want a classy wedding."

"How much for a band?"

"My cousin had a small combo playing at his wedding for twelve hundred. I'll put down a thousand. That's close."

"Patrick, what about the cake? The flowers? The food?"

For the next hour, we haggled. We gave up on an engagement announcement, the tuxedo, the wine, and chose the cheapest invitations we could find. We got the ring down to

$50, the photographer down to $600, the flowers down to the bridal bouquet and a couple of bouquets at the altar, and we settled on a store-bought cake from the Giant. There was just enough money left for a cold buffet in the church basement.

"This really stinks," said Patrick. "El cheapo wedding."

"Well, that's not supposed to matter if we really love each other," I said.

"It's just a horrible way to start a marriage, that's all, knowing you had to settle for cut-rate everything."

I stretched out my legs. "My dad said he spent his honeymoon in a tent. They camped out."

"Well, my folks went to Paris," said Patrick.

It was the first time Patrick sounded a bit grand to me. Sort of a snob. All he said was "my folks went to Paris," and somehow it made me mad.

"Well, I'd rather spend my honeymoon in a tent with the man I love than go to Paris with a snob," I snapped.

As soon as the words were out of my mouth, I regretted it. Actually, Patrick is one of the nicest, kindest guys I know, but there in my living room, talking about the wedding-that-wasn't, he sounded like a snob.

Patrick didn't say a word. He just looked at me for a long moment, then quietly gathered up his papers, thrust them in his notebook, stuck his pen in his pocket, and stood up.

"The wedding's off," he said, and went home.

• • •

I was crying before he ever got down the front steps. I don't even know if he said good-bye to Dad on the swing. This was ridiculous, but what was I going to tell Mr. Everett? I ran upstairs, dragging the hall phone into my room with me, and collapsed on the bed.

"Pamela!" I sobbed. "P-Patrick broke our engagement!"

"Alice? I can hardly hear you," came the voice at the end of the line.

"He b-broke the engagement!" I bleated, with scarcely breath enough to say the word. "The wedding's off!"

"Whose? Your dad's and Miss Summers's?"

"No! They're not engaged."

"Lester and Marilyn?"

"P-Patrick!" I almost shouted.

There was a pause. "What are you talking about? He's not going to do the assignment?"

"He-he's going to tell Mr. Everett the wedding's off."

"Great! So you *both* flunk! What happened?"

"We argued about everything!"

"But it's only an assignment!"

"I know, but . . . he said it was an el cheapo wedding, and I called him a snob and he left."

"You want to trade?" said Pamela. "I'll be the jilted bride, and you can be the pregnant teenager."

I wasn't exactly eager to do that. What if Pamela *did* have to go to a doctor and have a pelvic?

"Alice, don't you see this is what the assignment's

about—learning to face stuff like this before it really happens?" Pamela said.

"But he's never called me cheap."

"You never called him a snob, either. Listen, just type in all the figures you've collected so far and Mr. Everett will understand."

"But we haven't planned the honeymoon yet! We haven't shopped for furniture."

"Maybe Mr. Everett will let you go to divorce court instead," said Pamela. "What can I say?"

Both Dad and I were quiet at the table that night. Lester was getting ready to go over to Marilyn's for his special birthday dinner, and he came out in the kitchen to ask if we had any window washing fluid to put in his car.

"In the toolshed," Dad said, gazing off into space.

I sat leaning my head against my hand and played with my spaghetti.

"Well, this is a jolly little affair," Lester said when he came back in. He looked from Dad to me.

Dad blinked and immediately straightened up. "Guess I do feel pretty washed out," he said. "I spent the afternoon picking apples with Sylvia, and I'm pooped."

Lester rolled up the cuffs of his shirt and concentrated on me. "Is it my imagination, or have you been crying your eyes out all day over a lost love?"

"It's not funny, Lester."

"You *have* been crying your eyes out for a lost love?"

"Patrick called the wedding off," I said.

Both Dad and Lester stared at me.

"He said all we could afford was an el cheapo wedding. He wanted a honeymoon in Paris, and all we could afford was a weekend in a budget motel."

"Oh, I love this teacher! I *love* this teacher!" said Dad, suddenly coming to life. "Mr. Everett deserves an immediate raise in salary and promotion to supervisor. He's a genius."

Lester pulled out a chair and sat down. "I can't understand why you're so uptight over an assignment," he told me.

"It's the *way* we argued," I said. "We made each other mad."

"Well, kiddo, if Patrick hasn't called by the time I get back from Marilyn's, I'll be surprised. He's probably feeling as sorry about it as you are."

"Hey, that's right, it's your birthday, Les, and we haven't given you your presents yet," said Dad.

"Well, he's just about to get one." I gave Lester a look. I still didn't like the idea of Marilyn cooking for him in her underwear.

But Dad's thoughts were somewhere else. "You know, I was thinking this morning that I now have a twenty-one-year-old son, and if Marie were here, this would be a grand celebration."

"I was thinking of Mom this morning, too, as a matter of fact," Lester said. "Do you remember the way she always

brought a Kleenex to the table when she carried in a birthday cake with candles?"

Dad look puzzled a moment. "Now that you mention it,
I guess I do."

"I always thought it was because she was emotional about
our growing up and had a tissue ready in case she cried,"
Lester said. "I didn't find out till much later that the smoke
from the candles always set off her allergies, and that's why
she blew her nose."

We all laughed, even me. I wished I'd been older when
Mom died and had known her a little better so that I would
have stories to tell, too.

"She'd shop all year for your presents," Dad said.
"January, June, October, it didn't make any difference. If she
saw something she thought either of you would like, she'd
buy it and put it away."

"I remember how she used to let me lick the frosting pan
when she made our birthday cake. If it was our birthday, we
always got to lick the pan," I said, glad I had one thing to
contribute.

"She did?" said Lester.

"That was Aunt Sally, Al, not your mother," Dad told me.
"Marie liked to bake, but for some reason she always bought
a birthday cake at the bakery and had it decorated special."

"Oh," I said. I always do that. Aunt Sally took care of us
for a while after Mom died, and I always mix them up.

"Anyway, happy birthday, Les. I've got a few little presents here for you," Dad said, and went into the other room to get them. He came back with a certificate for some CDs from the Melody Inn and two denim sport shirts that looked like silk.

"Hey! Great taste, Dad! I love that faded look!" Lester said.

Dad gave me a glance, meaning it was my turn.

"I already gave him my present this morning," I said.

"She did?" Dad asked, turning to Lester.

"Don't ask," Les said, and got up. "Well, Marilyn wanted me there by eight."

"Happy birthday, anyway," I told him. "Now that you're twenty-one, you're officially a man."

The phone rang at that moment, so I went out in the hall to answer.

It was Patrick.

"Alice, I'm sorry about this afternoon," he said. "Let's elope."

4

A BALCONY, A JACUZZI, AND YOU

*P*atrick and I agreed that we'd had a dumb argument, and he said he'd be over the next afternoon to finish our assignment. Lester passed me as I hung up the phone, and five minutes after he'd left for Marilyn's, the phone rang again.

It was Crystal Harkins, another of Lester's girlfriends.

"Hi, Crystal!" I said. "I haven't talked to you for a couple of months." I really like Crystal, almost as much as Marilyn. Lester could marry either one of them and I'd be happy.

"I trust Les still has my number," she said, her voice flat.

Uh oh, I thought.

"Is he there, Alice? I wanted to wish him happy birthday."

I hesitated. "Well, not exactly," I said.

"You mean he's half there and half not?"

"I mean he was here just a couple of minutes ago, and now he's out celebrating his birthday with . . . some of his friends."

Silence.

Crystal can read me like a book. "*Some* of his friends, Alice?"

My mind whirred. Would Marilyn go to all the trouble to cook a big dinner just for Lester? Wouldn't it be natural to invite some of his friends?

"I'm pretty sure," I said. Then I remembered how she'd be cooking surf and turf in her bikini and possibly not much else. "Well, maybe not," I said.

"Alice, you can level with me. I really need you to be truthful, because I have some big decisions to make. Is Les out with Marilyn Rawley or not?"

I could honestly say no, because they weren't *out*. They were at Marilyn's.

"No, they're not out," I said.

Silence again.

"Are they *in*?"

"In *here,* you mean?"

"No, *in,* as in over-at-Marilyn's?"

I sighed. "Yeah, that's where he is, Crystal."

"Thank you, Alice. That's all I wanted to know."

"Crystal, wait!" I said.

"No, *Lester* can wait! He can wait until a hot day in January, as far as I'm concerned."

"What did he *do?*" I had to know.

"I told Lester a month ago I'd like to do something special for his birthday. A gourmet dinner or something."

Another home-cooked meal? If Lester had played his cards right, he could have eaten out almost every day that week.

"Maybe he forgot," I offered.

"That's the point, the whole point. He was supposed to let me know whether he wanted it on Friday or Saturday night. He didn't even have the decency to call."

"What were you going to wear?" I asked. I was wondering if he liked Marilyn's costume better.

"What difference does *that* make?" asked Crystal.

"I mean, were you going to cook in a special costume, or just wear jeans, or what?"

"Why would I wear a special costume?" said Crystal. "Who does he think he is? The king of Siam?" She and Elizabeth could be soul sisters. "Anyway, Alice, it's not your fault. I like you a lot and I always will."

"I like you, too, Crystal," I told her.

"And you know what? Lester's being at Marilyn's tonight may be the best thing that ever happened to me. Just tell him that I called to wish him a happy birthday, and there's a present on the way. All right?"

"Sure. I'll tell him," I said. "That's really nice of you, Crystal."

"Not necessarily," she said, and hung up.

Maybe Lester should have taken a course from Mr. Everett, I thought. Half his problems came about because he didn't plan ahead. How did he expect to stay friends with Crystal if he only took her out now and then? And how could he ever hope that Marilyn would marry him if he was still seeing Crystal at all?

Perhaps the problems of the world, in fact, were due to

poor planning. People having more babies than they could feed. Farmers buying land on the flood plains. People smoking and getting cancer. It hit me all of a sudden that what I was going to get in Mr. Everett's class, maybe, was the secret of life.

Patrick came over on Sunday.

"Got your suitcase packed?" he said, grinning.

Dad was reading the Sunday *Post* on the couch.

"Hello, Mr. McKinley, it's your future son-in-law again," Patrick said.

Dad lowered the paper.

I laughed. Maybe it was just my imagination, but Patrick's voice sounded deeper, more grown up.

"I hope you'll be very happy," said Dad, giving him a sardonic smile.

We needed a table, and Patrick likes to be near food, so we chose the kitchen. I gave him a bag of pretzels, and he pulled a chair over to my side.

This time we stuck with it. It wasn't the ideal wedding Patrick wanted, and it wasn't mine, but we somehow worked up a simple ceremony, a small buffet reception, gown, ring, flowers, photographer, and music for a little under three thousand dollars. And we ended up going to Niagara Falls on a "honeymoon special," three days for nine hundred dollars, airfare included.

Now we had to find an apartment, then the furniture.

"After we pay the first month's rent, then what do we do?" I asked.

"We'll both have to work. What kind of job do you want?" said Patrick.

To tell the truth, that's not something I worry about a whole lot. I shrugged. "When I was little I wanted to be Smokey the Bear," I told him.

Patrick laughed and put his arm around me.

"Then I wanted to be a veterinarian. Once I thought about being a teacher. Also a chef. What do *you* want to be?"

"A marine biologist or a drummer," said Patrick. Just like that. "I probably wouldn't be able to earn a living as a drummer, though. I mean, I wouldn't be satisfied unless it was a really great band. So I'll probably be a marine biologist who plays the drums on the side."

Talk about planning!

"Patrick," I said. "How long have you known you wanted to be a marine biologist? Did you just wake up one morning and it hit you, or what?"

"When I was real small we went to Sea World, and I guess that's where it started. Then we were snorkeling over in Japan, and I saw all the fish and eels and things, and, well, I decided it would be really interesting. If I'm going to spend my life working, I want it to be something I like."

I was really envious of Patrick right then, but according to our assignment, we were both high school graduates without any special training, so on paper, at least, we were equal.

"Where would you want to work if you couldn't go on to college right away?" I asked. We had to write down *something*.

"Probably an aquarium store."

"And if I wanted to be a chef, I'd probably start out as a waitress," I told him.

We went back to the living room for the want ads, and read them in the kitchen over some apple cider Dad had brought back from the orchard.

We couldn't find any help wanted ads for aquarium stores at all. The closest we could come was clerk in a pet store for $4.25 an hour. We found some ads for waitress at $2.50 an hour plus tips.

I did some fast arithmetic. "If I got tips, Patrick, I'll bet I could make ten dollars an hour, which would mean that together we'd be making sixteen-fifty an hour or . . ." I scribbled some more. "Five hundred and seventy dollars a week! Wow!"

"You have to deduct taxes and insurance and stuff. It would probably only come to five hundred," he said. "Four hundred, even."

"That's still sixteen hundred dollars a month," I told him, figuring it out on Dad's calculator. "That's pretty good. What kind of an apartment should we get?"

We each wrote down what we wanted most in an apartment, so we wouldn't quarrel about it. I said a big kitchen where we could sit around the table the way Dad and Lester and I do at home. And I wanted two bathrooms and a guest bedroom so Dad or Lester could come to visit.

Patrick said it would have to have a balcony overlooking a park, a Jacuzzi, and a study.

We went through the ads again looking for apartments in Silver Spring. The only one we found that had everything we wanted rented for $1,700 a month.

"A *month!*" I choked. "That would take both our paychecks!"

We studied the assignment sheet again. When we made out a budget we had to consider rent, food, taxes, car, medical and dental expenses, clothes, utilities, repairs, phone, entertainment, and incidentals.

We gave up the Jacuzzi and got the rent down to $1,200. We gave up the study and the large kitchen, and got it down to $1,100. Patrick said we could move out to the country away from the capital area and our rent would go down, but our car expenses would go up. By giving up the spare bedroom and the balcony overlooking a park, *any* park, we got the rent down to $600.

We sat there staring glumly at the newspaper.

"I don't think we can afford to get married," Patrick said. "This leaves only five hundred bucks for furniture."

"We'd have to scrimp and save every single penny," I added.

"Or live on love," said Patrick. And then, because he already had his arm around me, he kissed me.

Do you know what I like most about kissing in eighth grade? The kisses aren't always the same. Up until now, a kiss was a quick embarrassment. Patrick would sort of put his hands on my shoulders—to hold me still, I guess—and then, plop! A wet kiss somewhere around my mouth, and he was gone.

Now he kissed me walking down the street at night, or sitting there in the kitchen, a sideways kiss. It seemed more natural. But just when I was beginning to feel *really* comfortable, he said, "Do you like me?"

"Of course!"

"Why don't you ever kiss *me*?" he said.

I stared at him and felt the color creeping up into my cheeks. "But I do! What do you think we just did?"

"I mean, you never start it."

I was really confused. "I didn't know . . . I mean, that you wanted me . . . that I was supposed . . ."

"It'd be nice," he said.

I blushed to the roots of my hair. "Maybe sometime I'll surprise you," I said.

"I like surprises," said Patrick.

I don't know how a day that started out so right could suddenly go so wrong. It was like a big cloud hanging over me—the idea that Patrick was waiting for me to kiss him.

I mean, how would I know when to do it? He's taller than

I am, and I'd have to reach up, and . . . there was a sinking feeling in my chest.

What if we were sitting out on the swing together and he didn't know I was trying to kiss him and suddenly turned his head away? What if I ended up kissing his neck?

What if we were walking out on the sidewalk at night and I tried to kiss him and he kept on walking? What if I tried to kiss him sometime and he said, "Not *now*, Alice!"

Suddenly I had just a hint of what it was like to be a boy, of all the things they go through. I don't know how they stand it.

When Dad and Lester came out in the kitchen finally to start dinner, I realized it was time for us to wind up the assignment.

"Well, we got a lot done," I told Patrick. "All we have left now is to work out the rest of the budget and buy furniture."

"Man, this is the longest assignment I ever had!" Patrick said.

"I do love that teacher, though!" said Dad from the refrigerator where he was getting out the lettuce.

"So does Elizabeth," I said, and as soon as it escaped my lips, I knew I shouldn't have told. "I mean, she thinks he's a good teacher," I said quickly.

"I had a crush on a teacher once," Lester told us. He was rinsing off chicken pieces under the faucet. "My French teacher. I spent all of seventh grade imagining what kind of underwear she wore."

"That's sick," I said.

"Oh, I think that's pretty normal for a twelve-year-old." Dad smiled.

"I put a Mars bar in her desk once with a note that said, 'For You,' only I didn't sign it," Lester went on. "I guess I figured she'd recognize my handwriting. I don't know if she did or not, but I went back to her room several times that day to check the wastebasket and see if the wrapper was there. It wasn't. I always wondered what she did with that candy."

We laughed, Patrick, too.

Dad invited Patrick to stay for dinner, but he said he had to go, so I walked to the front door with him. Then I remembered what he'd said about me kissing him. I felt sick all over again.

Lester and Dad could see us if they looked down the hall, so I didn't try to kiss Patrick at the door. I went out on the porch with him, but he was already starting down the steps. Was I supposed to reach out and grab him or what?

I made up my mind that no matter what, I was going to do it and get it over with. I couldn't have it hanging over me like that. I had to *plan* it. Planning was everything!

I went down the steps with him. When we got to the bottom I'd kiss him, I thought. My heart was beating double time. This was ridiculous! Every time I thought of doing it, I lost my nerve.

It was just like it had been back in third grade with

Donald Sheavers, when we were playing Tarzan out in the yard and he was supposed to kiss me. We were on this big sheet of cardboard we pretended was a raft, but every time he reached over to kiss me, I got the giggles and rolled off.

"Well, what are you doing, walking me home?" Patrick said.

I swallowed and kept going.

"If you walk me home, I'll have to walk you home again," he said. "This could go on all night."

"Oh, just as far as the corner." I gulped. "It's . . . it's really nice out."

"Yeah," said Patrick.

A car was coming. After it passed, I could hear another one. Then another. I couldn't kiss him while cars were coming!

I set my eye on the mailbox. When we got as far as the mailbox, I'd kiss him. No, it had to be *before* the mailbox, or we'd be standing right under the streetlight.

Ten more steps and I'll do it, I told myself.

We walked ten steps.

Twenty more steps and I'll do it, I said.

We walked twenty.

Patrick looked down at me once, and suddenly I just grabbed his arm, reached up, and kissed him—it was sort of on the side of his nose—and then, like a complete idiot, I turned and ran all the way back home. It must have been one of the stupidest things I ever did.

I ran up on the porch, and as I opened the door, I stumbled over something there on the doormat and fell into the hallway.

"Al?" said Dad from the kitchen.

I sat up, rubbing my shin.

"What happened?" he asked, coming down the hall.

I pointed to a box that was sitting askew in the doorway, and pulled it in after me.

There was a piece of paper taped to the top. All it said was, *Lester—Crystal.*

5

𝒟ISCOVERY

"*ℒ*ester," Dad called. "For you."

Lester ambled in from the other room and I pulled myself up off the floor, still rubbing my leg.

Lester looked down at the box.

"It must have just come," I said. "It wasn't there when I went down to the corner with Patrick."

Lester picked it up and took it into the living room, setting it on the coffee table. The note didn't say anything else—just, *Lester—Crystal.*

"Uh-oh," Lester said when he opened the box. Dad sat across the room, but I had my nose right over the box. And somehow I knew that Crystal was returning everything Lester had ever given her.

To begin with, on top was a photograph of Crystal and Lester together, and it had been torn right down the middle, so Crystal was on one half, Les on the other.

"Oh, Lester!" I said, and sat down beside him on the couch.

But Lester was sorting through the box of mementos, exclaiming over one, then another.

"Haven't seen this for a long time!" he said, holding up one of his shirts that Crystal had borrowed.

There was a half-bottle of perfume, a book of poems, a radio, a toy yacht, a glass zebra, leather gloves, earrings— lots of earrings—a Swatch watch, a camera, and a dried rose.

"What the heck?" said Lester, holding up the rose. "Why would she save this?"

"Lester," Dad said, "that woman has invested quite a bit of time in you."

"And we both enjoyed it," Lester told him. "What do you want me to do, Dad? Marry her, just because she's invested some time in me?"

"No, but when you get that close to a woman, and then drop her . . ."

"I didn't drop her, she dropped me. She's a wonderful person, and if it weren't for Marilyn, I might say, 'Crystal's the one.' But I just can't see myself giving up Marilyn. I've tried to be honest with both of them, but did you ever try telling that to a woman—that you're crazy about two women at the same time?"

Dad sighed. "No, I can't say that I ever did. And I can't think of any woman who would be pleased to hear it."

"Well, there you have it, then," said Lester.

Dad went back in the kitchen, but Lester whistled as he continued emptying the box. He certainly didn't seem very upset. Maybe planning is harder for some people than it is for others. Maybe with Crystal out of the picture, Lester didn't have any decisions left to make, and the whole thing was just one big relief.

He went on sorting through the stuff in the box. "She sent back the radio! Why would she do that? It's a perfectly good radio." He lifted out the sweater he'd given her once, then the watch. "Hey, Al, want a Swatch watch? You can have the perfume, too."

"Really?" I said. It was like Christmas.

Maybe it was because Patrick and I had just spent the whole afternoon together on budgets and money matters, but it suddenly occurred to me that if Lester broke up with a woman every two years and she returned all his presents, I would probably have enough sweaters, perfume, watches, cameras, radios, shirts, and jewelry to last me through high school and college.

"Someday, Les," I told him, "you should give a woman a really neat jacket—you know, the kind that looks like silk and has designs and colors all over it?"

"Why?"

"Because I would look great in it," I said. I nudged him. "How was the surf and turf last night?"

"Pretty good. Marilyn's a great cook."

"How was the costume?"

"Terrific."

I tried to think how I could get more information from him. "What I can't understand is how she could cook a whole dinner just wearing boots and a bikini. I mean, she could have burned her—"

"Oh, she only wore the boots for about ten minutes, then gave them up and went barefoot," said Lester.

I wasn't the only one wearing something new to school the next day. I had on the Swatch watch, the sweater, and a pair of Crystal's earrings, but Elizabeth was wearing a short black skirt over black tights, and a blue lacy knit top that you were supposed to wear without anything underneath, but Elizabeth had on a bra (a sports bra, if you want the truth). Not only that, but her hair was different. She'd braided it up into a fancy ponytail. She told me once she wanted to be a nun. I doubted it.

"Do I detect a little blue eyeshadow?" asked Pamela as we got on the bus.

I looked closely, too. "And a little mascara? Maybe Raspberry Creme lip gloss?"

"It's just a change," Elizabeth said. "Who wants the same old look every day?"

Pamela and I exchanged glances.

It's weird, but this time in health class I really paid attention to what was going on besides the lesson. Elizabeth wasn't the only girl who was playing up to Mr. Everett.

Jill and Karen and a number of other girls had been hanging around his desk when I came in, and now that class had started, they just sat in their seats smiling at him. No matter what he said, no matter how serious, they had those stupid smiles on their faces. Every time he said something remotely funny, they laughed out loud.

Then I remembered that ever since school had started, they'd teased him about something.

They teased him about his tie.

They teased him about his hair, the way it hung down in his face.

He told them to go sit down, and they even giggled about that.

I don't know. I've never gone nuts over people who don't really know me from vanilla pudding. It would be hard, for example, even to pretend that Michael Jackson has the least little interest in me, even if he were to give me his autograph. I've never gone in much for pining over people I can't have. Except my mom, of course.

"Okay, who's having problems?" Mr. Everett was saying. "How are the assignments going? Any questions?"

Jill had her hand in the air. "I want to trade my situation with someone else."

"What was your assignment?"

"I have to arrange a funeral for my grandmother."

"Sorry," said Mr. Everett. "No trading."

"I hardly even *know* my grandmother," Jill protested. "If she died, somebody else would bury her or she wouldn't get buried at all."

The class laughed.

"Listen, Jill, someday somebody close to you is going to die, and it may be when you least expect it. Your job is to find out what types of burials are available, what alternatives there might be, expenses—the whole works—and to share your information with the class."

"It's boring, Mr. Everett! It's depressing!" Jill complained.

"So's life sometimes," he told her.

"But what does it have to do with health?"

"It has a lot to do with mental health, and that's just as important as the way we treat our bodies."

Elizabeth didn't lean on his desk the way the other girls did. Actually, she didn't do anything especially flirtatious at all, she just never took her eyes off Mr. Everett. She sat there with her lips half-parted as though our teacher were flexing his muscles in a nylon bikini. She didn't take notes. She didn't read his handouts. If I'd walked over and passed my hand back and forth in front of her face, I doubt she would have blinked.

"Is it really over between you and Tom Perona?" I asked her on our way to study hall.

"He's so childish," she said. "I'm looking for someone more mature."

I missed having Miss Summers for English. She teaches both seventh- and eighth-grade English, but I was assigned to Mr. Tawes, so I didn't get to drink in her wonderful perfume or admire the way she blends colors and fabrics and makes them work. I didn't get to daydream about what it would be like if she were my stepmother and I got to hug her every day. I'd only seen her a few times since school started, in fact, passing in the hall or moving through the cafeteria at lunchtime.

"Hi, Alice," she'd say, smiling her beautiful smile, and I'd remember the time she leaned against our piano and sang while Dad played, or the day we baked Dad's birthday cake at her house to surprise him.

"When is your dad going to marry her?" Pamela asked at lunchtime, just before I was condemned to another of Mr. Tawes's boring lectures.

"I'll be the last to know," I said. "I haven't seen very much of her lately, so I'm not sure what's happening. They're awfully private about everything."

"What's 'everything'?" Pamela said with a grin.

"Pamela!" Elizabeth snapped. At least underneath that lacy top and fancy ponytail, she was the same old Elizabeth.

"She hasn't even been to our house in the last few months," I said. "Dad goes over there."

"Naturally! That proves it, then," said Pamela. "She lives alone. What could they do with you and Lester around?"

"Everything is sex to you, Pamela. There's a lot more to relationships than that," Elizabeth told her.

We looked at Elizabeth.

"How would *you* know?" asked Pamela. "You and Tom Perona only lasted a week."

Elizabeth ignored her. "You can have a deep meaningful relationship with someone just by looking into his eyes, just knowing that he understands."

Uh-oh, I thought again.

"Would we be speaking of anyone in particular?" asked Pamela.

"I'm just making a point," Elizabeth told us.

She wanted to use the rest room off the west corridor after lunch, however, because we had to pass Mr. Everett's room to get there. And sitting by her on the bus home that afternoon, I noticed that there were strange drawings—doodles, sort of—all over her notebook cover, and then I realized that it was the word "Everett" written horizontally, vertically, diagonally, the *r* in the middle being the same *r* for them all. All over her notebook, there were those little star-shaped diagrams that looked like snowflakes, but when you examined them closely, turned out to be more "Everetts."

I was afraid that Elizabeth might do something really stupid, like write Mr. Everett a love note that she'd be embarrassed about later. I decided I'd go see Miss Summers at school the next day and ask if any boy had ever had a crush on her and what she did about it. She'd probably have some good suggestions.

Every teacher in our school has a "catch-up" period during the day, forty minutes to do paperwork or plan assignments. It's also a time that any student needing extra help can schedule a conference. Last semester Miss Summers had her planning period just before lunch, so I got a pass during study period and went up to her room to see if this was still her free time.

It's weird when the halls are empty. When you have a pass to leave class, you get to see what the building really looks like, because during class changes the corridors are filled with students. The halls are noisy and choked with arms and elbows, and if you round a corner too sharply, especially near the gym, you're in danger of losing your life.

As I went up the stairs to the second floor, I realized I hadn't even checked once since school started to see if Miss Summers was wearing a diamond. I figure Dad might not tell me right away if they were engaged, but a ring would. In seventh grade, when she was my teacher, I used to check every day.

Don't forget to check her finger, I told myself as I reached the landing at the top and went down the hall toward Room 202.

I was within a couple of feet of the doorway when I heard voices coming from inside and I stopped. *Darn!* I'd been hoping she would be alone.

". . . just don't badger me." It was Sylvia Summers's voice. A personal, not a professional, voice.

I stood dead still.

And then a man's: "I'm *not* badgering you."

"Yes, you are, Jim. Just asking me what I'll be doing when you already know I have plans is a form of badgering."

I felt as though there were ice water in my veins. Where had I heard that man's voice? Who was she talking to?

I didn't dare go to the doorway to find out. It sounded as though they were standing just inside. I knew that I should hightail it out of there, but I couldn't. I just couldn't. I backed up against the lockers and strained to hear more.

Now the voices were too indistinct to make out what they were saying. A murmur. Then another. Then: "Sylvia, I have to know."

"Why? You were able to go very well a whole year without anything being resolved. Why now, when *I've* met someone?"

My heart was pounding. *Yes!* She must be referring to Dad. Why didn't she say "someone wonderful" or "someone special"?

"Because I thought we had an understanding. Yes, I realized we could each meet someone new, and I'm willing now to be patient, up to a point, but—"

"Then be patient," Miss Summers said.

Silence. Even out in the hallway, I could sense the tension. They weren't kissing. I knew that without looking.

"For how long? A month? Six months? A year?"

"However long it takes. I have to sort things out."

"Sylvia, answer this: Are you sure you don't just like the idea of playing mommy?"

"I'm not playing, Jim."

"No. I was afraid you'd say that. . . ."

I couldn't take anymore. As much as I wanted to stay and hear the rest, I was too afraid, I guess, of what it might be. I moved down the hall to the drinking fountain and stopped, resting my hands on both sides of it. And as soon as the man came striding out the doorway, I leaned over the fountain and he walked on by. Mr. Sorringer, the vice-principal!

I couldn't go to Miss Summers's room now. I felt as though I could never go there again. There was a lump in my throat as large as a Ping-Pong ball. I kept holding on to the sides of the fountain, and everything came together in my head, little pieces of puzzle falling into place: the fact that Mr. Sorringer had spent last year in California getting his degree; that Miss Summers had gone to California to spend Christmas; that she told me she was "very fond"of my dad, but she never said "love"; that she and Dad still weren't engaged; that I had seen her and the vice-principal together in a restaurant when Lester took me out to dinner; that she and Dad hadn't been seeing each other as much as they used to, and that Dad had been so thoughtful lately. Depressed, I think.

Shock gave way to sadness—for Dad, for me, for Lester. And then I felt angry.

She *had* to make up her mind. I couldn't stand this any longer. Neither could Dad. What would it take to convince her she had already met the most wonderful man in the world, and if she said no to my father, she would be miserable the rest of her life? How could any woman *not* like my dad?

I turned all my anger onto Mr. Sorringer. *Mr. Sorringer, I hate you!* I whispered.

• • •

We made a real pair, Elizabeth and me. For the rest of the week she went out of her way to walk by Mr. Everett's room, and I went out of my way to avoid Sylvia Summers. After world studies, I'd circle the whole building rather than pass her room to get to my locker. I was afraid that anything I might do or say would convince her to marry the vice-principal instead of Dad. I didn't want the responsibility. When I saw her coming, I'd turn down a side corridor or duck into the rest room.

At home, Dad seemed even more quiet than usual. When we did the dishes together, I saw him washing the same pan over and over, and had to reach out and take it from him.

Finally I went up to Lester's room, where he was typing a college paper.

"Lester," I said, "I need to talk."

I came in and sat on the edge of his bed. He was typing, but he slowed down enough to hear me.

"I'm afraid she'll marry that guy, Les," I said after telling him what I'd overheard. "It will just kill Dad if she does. What can we do?"

"Mind your own business, Al. You can help Dad the most by not asking questions, not interfering, and certainly by not saying anything to Sylvia."

I knew he was right. No amount of planning on my part would bring Dad and Miss Summers any closer together. I also knew that keeping quiet would be one of the hardest things I had ever done in my life.

6

NEW GIRL AT THE STORE

When I went to the Melody Inn on Saturday, Janice Sherman, in sheet music, asked if I would go with her during lunch hour to buy a wedding gift for Loretta Jenkins, who runs our Gift Shoppe. Loretta Jenkins James, actually.

Loretta, whose wild curly hair is like a sunburst around her head, got married a few weeks ago without telling anyone. Except her new husband, of course, and the justice of the peace. Well, actually, she got pregnant first, and then she got married. She spent her honeymoon throwing up.

So the wedding gift was also to be a shower gift and a going-away present, because Loretta had only been to work nine times in the last three weeks, and finally decided she would rather throw up in her own bathroom than in the rest room here at work. In her mother-in-law's bathroom, I mean, because she and her husband had to move in with his folks. She said she wanted to stay home with the baby anyway after it was born, so she gave Dad two weeks' notice. This was her last day.

"Sure, I'll go with you," I said to Janice.

Janice reminds me of a banker, because she wears suits and scarves or little string ties. Her glasses dangle from a chain around her neck, and all she really needs is a watch in a vest pocket to complete the picture. She used to date one of our trombone instructors, but since they broke up, she's had her eye on Dad again. The one person I know for sure I do not want for a stepmother is Janice Sherman.

After I filed some sheet music and put price stickers on a stack of yellow instruction books called *Keyboard Sonatas for Four Hands,* which sounds as though they were written for freaks, I went across the store and back under the mezzanine where we sell guitar picks, violin strings, banjo tuners, and trumpet mutes, along with a big selection of musical gifts.

My favorite job in the whole store is cleaning the glass on the gift wheel. You press a button and the wheel goes around, and when you see a pair of earrings in the shape of clef signs or tiny gold trumpets and you want to try them on, you can stop the wheel and Loretta will take them out for you. Except that Loretta wasn't there. From where I stood in the Gift Shoppe, I could hear her vomiting back in the stockroom. Dad said maybe it was a good thing this was her last day.

I waited until she came out, pale-faced and thinner than when I'd seen her last. She gave me a wan smile.

"If this is what pregnancy is like, you wonder how there are so many people in the world, huh?" she said.

I smiled back. "Pretty awful, huh?"

"Mornings are the worst. But sometimes afternoons are bad and there are even a few evenings that are awful. I've got girlfriends, though, who say they went the whole nine months and didn't upchuck once. I should be so lucky."

"What's he like? Your husband?"

"Cute. A little crazy. If you'd asked me four months ago if I would ever marry a bartender and live with his parents, I would have said no, but here I am."

I shouldn't have asked, but I did. "Loretta, are you sorry?"

"Why should I be sorry? What will be will be. I just take it as it comes, Alice."

Do you know what I was thinking just then? I was thinking I should take her to Mr. Everett's class as Exhibit A. How could you end up being married to a man you didn't expect to marry, living in a place you didn't really want to be, with a baby coming you didn't plan for, and not wonder if this was really what you wanted?

After I'd put in my three hours, Janice and I went to lunch together and then shopping. Since neither of us had ever been married or had a baby, it was sort of the blind leading the blind. We ended up buying a wind chime of little baby angels made of white cappa shells and tiny gold harps.

The baby angels were for the baby Loretta was going to have, the harps were a reminder of the Melody Inn, and the wind chime itself was to hang in Loretta's new home, which happened to be her in-laws'. We had the store gift wrap it, and then we went back to the Melody Inn and gave it to Loretta.

Dad said how much he appreciated her work here at the Gift Shoppe, and gave her an envelope with an extra week's pay in it. Loretta had barely said thank you when she had to rush back to the toilets again, and Dad said why didn't she take the rest of the day off, so she took the wind chime and went home.

"Well!" said Dad, after she'd gone. "Janice, what do we do now?"

"I've got two applicants lined up already. The word must have been getting around that Loretta was leaving," Janice told him.

"You're wonderful," Dad said.

Later that evening I began to worry. Saturday night, and Dad was puttering around the house when he should have been out with Miss Summers. Not only that, but he seemed distracted. He'd pick up part of the newspaper and start to read it, then lay it down. Five minutes later he'd read the same page all over again.

I was standing in the dining room eating an apple, and finally I walked over and sat beside him on the couch.

"What's the matter, Dad? Problems?"

He let out his breath. "All life is a problem, Al."

"Anything in particular?"

Dad looked over at me and gave me a little grin. "Who are you, my analyst?"

"I just wondered. You seem a little down."

"Oh, honey, I'm just an old man who feels he's out of his depth, sometimes."

"Come on, Dad."

He reached over and slapped my knee. "Okay, Doc McKinley, I'll snap out of it."

I gave him a hug, but still didn't leave.

"Dad," I said finally. "No matter what happens, please don't marry Janice Sherman."

"What brought that on?"

"I just don't want Janice Sherman for a stepmother."

"It never would have entered my mind," he told me.

At school, as people began turning in their preliminary reports for the unit on Critical Choices, Mr. Everett spent class time talking about them.

"Okay, Brian, let's look at yours," Mr. Everett said. "You total your car and you're charged with DWI. How much alcohol did you drink?"

"How should I know? I was too drunk to know my own name."

Everyone laughed.

"He was at a chug-a-lug party," one of the boys called out, and we laughed some more.

Mr. Everett began scribbling notes on Brian's paper. "I

want to know exactly how much wine it takes to put you over the legal limit, how much beer, how much whiskey, the works. Now down here, you say you went to court. What day did you go?"

"Huh?" said Brian. "What does it matter?"

"It matters. You think it's going to be a nice convenient Saturday, maybe? I want to know what day, I want to know how you got there. . . ."

"How I *got* there?"

"You weren't foolish enough to drive with a suspended license, were you? And when they didn't get to your case the day you were supposed to go in, I want to know how many more times you had to take off school or take off work and have your dad take off work to drive you there."

"They call you in and don't get to your case?"

"Check it out," said Mr. Everett, handing his paper back. "You've got a lot more work to do here."

Mr. Everett was no pushover, and we knew it.

Patrick had been busy after school all week getting ready for a track meet that weekend, and if he wasn't at the track, he was at band practice. I was just as glad, because I found myself avoiding him since the night I'd kissed him by the mailbox. I had just been so incredibly silly about it, like a six-year-old instead of a thirteen-year-old.

But after class on this particular day, Patrick caught up with me in the hall and slipped his arm around my waist.

"Hey, you aren't avoiding me, are you? I thought we were engaged," he said.

I laughed then, but I still felt embarrassed. "Well, when do you want to work some more on our assignment?" I asked.

"What do we have to do next?"

"Go furniture shopping."

"Next week is going to be murder. The week after? We'll still make the deadline."

"Okay."

We took a few steps more.

"That was some kiss," he went on.

I turned away. I could feel my face blushing.

"Next time, try to get the upper lip. You were sort of heavy on the nose."

"Patrick!"

"See you," he said, and turned the corner.

It was Lester's night to cook, and he was making my favorite, black bean burritos with purple onions and cheese. I could smell the beans heating as soon as I got in the house.

"For a minute, there, I thought you were Crystal," Les said.

I was wearing her sweater again, her earrings, her watch, her perfume. I put my books down on the table. "Is it really over between you, Lester?"

He shrugged. "Until she asks for her presents back, I guess it is."

"What?"

"Relax, Al. They're yours. Besides, she's been out the last couple times I've called. Either that or she's avoiding me."

I got down a box of crackers and stood by the table eating a handful. Whenever Lester looked my way, I chewed with my mouth open just to annoy him. He says it was my most disgusting habit as a young kid, so I have to do it occasionally to test his reaction time. He passed. He immediately made a gagging reflex.

"Lester," I said, "do you think you'll ever marry?"

"When I'm sixty, maybe."

"Do you *plan* your life? I mean, do you know what you'll be doing after graduation?"

"I don't even know what I'll be doing Saturday night," he told me.

"In Mr. Everett's class we're learning to plan."

"Bully for you. If you can plan when you fall in love, you've got it made. Make sure it's about three years after you graduate from college, so you can have a good job and some savings. Plan when you're going to take a vacation so it won't be the same week it's going to rain. Plan not to get sick when you've got a big event coming up, and of course you don't want to die till you've accomplished everything you've got on your list, so you'll want to set a date for checkout."

"You don't believe in planning, Lester?"

"In the words of the Scottish poet Robert Burns, 'The best laid schemes o' mice an' men gang aft a-gley.'"

"Huh?" I said.

"It means that no matter how well you plan something, it often doesn't work out due to circumstances beyond your control."

"Thanks a lot," I said. And then, "Do you think that if Dad and Miss Summers don't marry, he'll end up with Janice Sherman?"

"Why should you care?"

"Les, can you imagine Janice Sherman in our house? She'd have all the spices alphabetically arranged. She'd have everything in the freezer labeled. She'd even put name tags on our underwear."

"If he marries Janice, I'm outa here," said Lester.

"You can't," I told him. "As my older brother, it's your responsibility to stick around till I've finished college or married or both. That's what I heard."

"Well, kiddo, you heard wrong. If you decide not to marry or go to college, I'm stuck here forever?"

I sighed. "I wish I knew the future."

"No, you don't. That would take all the fun out of life. Believe me, Al."

Dad came home about six-thirty, and as he washed his hands at the sink, he said, "I've got news."

I sat up perfectly straight. "You and Miss Summers are engaged?"

He gave me a strained look, and I was immediately sorry I'd said it. "No, Al. Actually, I guess it's not news so much as a question." He sat down across from us. "Janice has two applicants lined up for Loretta's job. Both are good, but one is stupendous. Really knows her music. Which one do I hire?"

"Is this a trick question?" asked Lester, taking a big bite of burrito and pushing it over to one side of his mouth as he chewed. "What's to decide?"

"The stupendous one is Marilyn Rawley."

Lester choked. "*What?*"

"I was as surprised as you are. Janice wasn't even aware that we knew her."

"But . . . but she goes to school! She's in one of my classes!"

"Part-time," Dad said. "It's a drawback, but we could work around it. She has several evening classes this semester, evidently, so it would be only one morning and two afternoons a week we'd have to fill in without her. I think we could swing it. The big plus is that when she *is* there, she could help out in other departments. She is much more knowledgeable than Loretta was."

"Then what's the problem?" I asked.

Dad chewed thoughtfully. "I'm just not sure it's wise to have her working for me. What happens if you two break up, Lester? What happens if you break her heart? What happens if she breaks yours?"

"My heart is made of surgical steel," said Lester.

"That's what you think," Dad told him.

I imagined going to the Melody Inn on Saturdays and

working beside Marilyn in the Gift Shoppe. I imagined having woman-to-woman talks and telling her all my secrets and listening to hers.

"Hire her, Dad! Please!" I said. "I *love* Marilyn. I'd love to work with her. She knows all about music. She plays the guitar and sings. She sang in the *Messiah,* and all the customers would love her."

Dad looked at Lester.

"Hire her," said Les.

"Okay," said Dad. "I just wanted your input first."

I couldn't stop grinning. If I wasn't getting a mother, maybe I was getting a sister-in-law. And if I wasn't getting a sister-in-law, maybe I was getting a sister.

$\mathscr{O}$N PAMELA AND PREGNANCY

$\mathscr{A}$ccording to Pamela's assignment, she could be as pregnant as she wanted, but had to report on what choices she would need to make, based on how many months she was along. She also had to report on the possible consequences of whatever she decided to do about her unborn child.

We had figured out by this time that Mr. Everett was going to grade us on just how many factors we considered. If he saw we were choosing the easy way out and taking the first solution that came into our heads, he'd add twenty more things to research.

Pamela called some clinics who told her that if she was thinking about an abortion, they'd only perform it in the first three months, and, depending on what state she lived in, she'd have to have her parents' permission.

If she made up her mind to have the baby, she had to decide whether to keep it or give it up for adoption. And while there were a lot of infertile couples who would lovingly adopt a healthy newborn, the strikes were against it if it had a handicap.

"Okay, I'll be six months pregnant," Pamela informed me on the school bus one morning. "I decided to choose the month I'd really be showing."

"You just wanted to skip all the morning sickness," said Elizabeth, who knows whereof she speaks, because her mom's expecting at the end of October.

Pamela had to figure out where she would live, where she would work, and whether or not to finish high school, and make as many other decisions as she could cram into her report.

"What I found out," she said to me, while Elizabeth hung over the back of the seat, "is if I name the father, they can force him to provide child support. If he's working, that is. But I might not want to. I might be afraid that if they go after him for child support, he'll never marry me."

"Every baby needs a father," said Elizabeth. "Why wouldn't they *make* you tell?"

"How?" I asked. "Stick hot pins in her thumbs till she confesses?"

"I could just say I didn't know," Pamela told us.

"How could you *not* know?" Elizabeth demanded.

"Maybe I was drunk at a party and there were too many guys to count."

"That's disgusting!" cried Elizabeth.

"I know, but it happens," Pamela told her.

"Then who should we say is the father?" I asked. "Brian? Mark?"

Pamela grinned. "I'm going to name Donald Sheavers."

"Oh, Pamela, no!" I giggled. Donald was my old boyfriend back in Takoma Park. We met him in the mall last summer, and he's been calling Elizabeth and Pamela ever since. "If it's Donald Sheavers's baby, it will be handsome as anything, but dumb as a doorknob."

"I don't think we should even be talking like this," said Elizabeth.

"It's all in *fun!*" I said. "Lighten up."

Elizabeth sighed, her arms resting on the back of our seat. "You know when I wish I had lived? Back in troubadour times."

"In what?" I asked.

"When the troubadours lived. The men who sang to ladies who lived in castles. They made up love songs, and the women looked down on them lovingly and dropped their handkerchiefs so the troubadours would have a token of their love, and the troubadours went on wandering, and forever after, women would have this memory of unconsummated love."

"What's the *point?*" asked Pamela.

"The *point* is that you can cherish and love someone deeply, Pamela—*deeply*—without ever having to take your clothes off. It's love on a higher plane."

"Spare me!" said Pamela.

"Only very few people will ever experience this kind of love in their lifetime, because they let their bodies get in the way," Elizabeth went on.

There's just no reasoning with her sometimes.

• • •

After school, Pamela asked us to go with her to McDonald's to apply for a job. She had a list of other places that usually hire teenagers. She'd tell them she was six months' pregnant and see how many rejections she got. We figured how many places we could hit on or near Georgia Avenue that had been hiring now that their summer help was back in school.

"But if they say no, how can you prove it's because you're pregnant?" Elizabeth asked.

"Because one of you will go in first and fill out an application, and after you come out, I'll go in and ask if they're hiring. If they take your application but not mine, then we'll know."

"You don't look very pregnant," I told her. "You need a pillow."

"Come on over to my house, Pamela," Elizabeth said. "My mother will make you look *very* pregnant."

Mrs. Price herself looked very, very pregnant.

"Six months' pregnant, huh?" she asked Pamela. "Let's try a small flat decorator pillow, and see how that looks under a maternity top."

She bound it to Pamela's body with a long cotton scarf, then slipped a maternity top over Pamela's head.

We stared at the transformation.

"It . . . it looks so real!" gasped Elizabeth.

"It feels weird!" Pamela told us, patting her artificial abdomen.

It *was* weird. In Mr. Everett's course it was as though someone had put our lives on fast-forward.

Before we left the house for McDonald's, Mrs. Price said, "What you have to remember now, Pamela, is to sit and stand a little slower than usual, and rest one hand lightly on your tummy, as if to quiet the baby down. It does a lot of kicking, you know. Feels like giant hiccups in your abdomen. Pretend that every time you change position you're going to get a kick in the gut unless you do it slowly."

Pamela practiced a couple times.

"It doesn't hurt to huff and puff a little," said Elizabeth's mother.

We set out, but couldn't stop giggling. People looked at us, especially at Pamela. Especially her abdomen.

"This is so weird," Pamela kept saying, but I knew she was having fun.

"Just don't go into labor or try anything dumb," Elizabeth warned, not at all sure about it.

When we got to McDonald's, I went in first and asked if I could fill out an application. They handed one right over. I gave a phony name and age, of course, because I really don't want to work there.

Then we went to the diner, and Elizabeth asked for an application. After she filled hers out, we went back to McDonald's again, and stayed out of sight while Pamela went in. She was out within a minute.

"They said I could fill out an application, but I would find the work difficult because I'd be on my feet all day," she told us.

"At least they were honest," I said.

We went back to the diner. They told Pamela they were no longer hiring. We goofed around down the block for a while, and then I went in the diner and asked about work. They gave me an application.

When I came out, Karen and Jill had come along. All the girls were laughing down at the corner.

"This is so *neat!*" Karen kept saying. "Everybody's looking at you, Pamela. It's so real!"

"Everyone got a fun assignment except me," Jill complained.

"Let's head over to the library and see the reaction," said Karen, and when we walked up the steps, we saw Brian and some other guys coming out.

"Whooaaa!" said Brian, staring.

"Hey, Brian, you've been busy!" said one of his friends, and whooped.

"It's not yours, Brian, don't worry," Pamela kidded.

"Whose is it, then?" asked Brian.

Pamela shook her head. "My lips are sealed."

The boys followed us back inside and tried to make Pamela tell, but she wouldn't. Everyone looked at us. We tried not to laugh, but couldn't help it. Pamela moved slowly, one hand on her stomach, and when she sat down, she leaned back, her abdomen sticking out in front of her. By this time, though, the pillow had slipped to one side, and that made us hysterical.

A librarian came over. "Please?" she said.

We put our hands over our mouths as Pamela reached up under the maternity top and pulled the bulge forward again. The librarian stared. We couldn't help ourselves this time and got up and left before they kicked us out, laughing all the way.

Pamela told the class the next day about applying for jobs as a pregnant teenager.

"This is the kind of thing I'm looking for," Mr. Everett told the rest of us. "Approach your assigned situation as though it were really your personal problem, and try to think of all the people your decision is going to affect. I don't want any dumb speculation. I want you to experience what some of these situations would really mean for you. And I don't care if you have a little fun while you're at it." He grinned at Patrick and me. "You two excepted," he said.

When the bell rang that day and the others were leaving, I went to the back of the room to look up something in the legal encyclopedia that Mr. Everett keeps for reference. The one thing Patrick and I hadn't checked was how long it takes to get a marriage license in Maryland, and the cost. Jill was up at Mr. Everett's desk—Jill, who got the name "Colorado" in seventh grade when boys were naming girls after states based on the size of their breasts.

"It's not fair, Mr. Everett!" I heard her saying. "Pamela and everyone else got a fun assignment, and you gave me a dead grandmother. Almost anything would be better than that."

Mr. Everett was gathering up his papers. "Listen, Jill, you can't always choose what happens to you in life. It's important to see how you deal with this."

"*Please*, Mr. Everett!" She was using her whining voice. "It just isn't any fun at all."

"Fun is not the object here." He was smiling at her, but standing his ground.

"Mr. Ever-ett!" Jill wailed. She motioned vaguely at her breasts. "Look at me! I mean, I look a lot older than my age. You've got to admit that I'm going to be faced with a lot more serious problems than burying a grandmother."

I couldn't believe she'd said that, but Mr. Everett didn't give an inch: "Well, if you've got the body of a woman, then you have to be thinking about what kind of decisions women have to make. And somewhere along the way you'll have to bury someone. It's as important an assignment as any of the others."

He tucked his papers under one arm and gave her a quick hug with the other as he headed for the door.

"Come on now, Jill. You can do it," he said, and he was gone.

She glared after him, then stalked on out into the hall.

On Saturday morning when I went to the Melody Inn, there was Marilyn Rawley in the Gift Shoppe.

"Marilyn!" I said.

"Hi, Alice!" She smiled. "Can you believe this? I got the job! Lester mentioned that Loretta was leaving, and I thought, 'Hey, *that's* a job I could do!'"

"When Dad told us you had applied, we both said, 'Hire her!'" I said.

Marilyn looked at me. "Your dad asked you what he should do?"

"No! I mean, he already knew he wanted you. He said you were super-qualified. He just wanted us to know."

"Well, I'll get to see you every Saturday," she said as I set to work cleaning the glass on her display cases.

Already Marilyn had made changes. Loretta had always done the ordering before, so along with the Beethoven T-shirts, there were bikini briefs with a name of a composer on the seat of the pants, notepads with the words "Chopin Liszt"at the top of each page, a mug with a conductor on it who, when the cup was filled with hot coffee, lost his clothes.

All of those items had been placed on a back shelf, and the display case had been completely rearranged. Taking center stage was a music box with *The Phantom of the Opera* on top; a gold charm bracelet with miniature instruments dangling from it; a necklace made of clef signs; silk scarves with a green and silver harp motif; and boxes of notecards featuring scenes from the birthplaces of six famous composers. The store had suddenly taken on more class.

"It's lovely, Marilyn!" Janice Sherman told her.

"Should have done this long ago," Dad said.

Marilyn smiled and looked pleased.

"It will take me a little longer to finish school this way because I'll have to cut back on my courses, but at least I'll have some spending money on the side," she told me. "I'm tired of living at the poverty level."

I was taking my time cleaning the glass because I wanted to stay in the Gift Shoppe as long as possible that morning.

"What are you majoring in?" I asked her.

"Well, it's sort of a general course of study right now, with an emphasis on music. I don't think I want to teach music in schools. I'm not real good with lots of people at once, I'm better one-on-one. So I'm looking into music therapy in nursing homes, psychiatric wards—places where music can make a difference."

I wished I could take Marilyn to Mr. Everett's class as Exhibit B—thinking about your life in advance. I know I shouldn't have said it, but the question just slipped out: "Does a husband figure in any of these plans, Marilyn?"

She smiled back. "Life is full of surprises," she said. Which is about the way Lester would have put it.

Pamela, Elizabeth, Jill, Karen, and I went to Wheaton Plaza on Sunday afternoon, accompanied by the pillow pregnancy, just for the fun of it. Just to see if anything would happen that Pamela could put in her report.

We even went into a maternity shop and Pamela tried on

black slinky cocktail dresses for mothers-to-be. She came out of the dressing room to check herself in the three-way mirror, and the sales clerk told her how beautiful she looked and how romantic it would make her husband.

"Oh, she doesn't have a husband," Elizabeth said with a straight face.

The sales clerk stopped in her tracks.

"She's not even sure who the father is," I added.

The clerk backed off. She said to remember to dry-clean the dress and disappeared.

We met several kids from our class when we were going down the escalator, and soon we had grown to a group of ten. We were just passing the Orange Bowl when I saw Donald Sheavers. I nudged Elizabeth on one side, Pamela on the other, and as Donald came toward us, Pamela held out her arms dramatically and called, "Daddy!"

Donald stared. Other customers stopped and stared.

"Here he is!" Pamela cried. "The father of my child!"

Donald Sheavers will never be the same again.

$\mathscr{B}$ACKSEAT DRIVERS

$\mathscr{I}$ hadn't talked to Miss Summers, other than a "Hi" in the hallway, since the day I'd overheard her talking with our vice-principal.

She'd smile her warm smile, of course, and usually add a little something, like, "That's a great sweater," or "You must be keeping busy; I hardly see you anymore," but it never lasted longer than ten seconds.

But just when I'd about given up hope that she and Dad would become "an item," as Pamela put it, Dad mentioned that the Melody Inn was sponsoring a concert at Montgomery College to benefit the homeless, and that Miss Summers was helping design the posters. Maybe they were going to have one of those meaningful platonic relationships that Elizabeth talked about. Maybe my father was destined to be a troubadour who sang to his lady and loved her from afar. The best thing I could do, as Lester said, was keep my mouth shut.

But Mr. Sorringer was a different matter. I felt as though I hated the man. My algebra class was just down the hall from his office, and every time I saw him in the hallway, I stared straight ahead or right through him, even though he said hello. He was a friendly person who always talked to students, and once, when I was getting something from my locker and he passed with a "How you doing?" I just slammed the locker shut and walked on.

"How mature of you," Lester said later when I told him.

I couldn't help how I felt, though. If it weren't for him, Dad and Miss Summers might be married. Engaged, anyway. Every weekend she wasn't out with Dad, I figured she was out with Sorringer.

Aunt Sally called one night to see how Pamela's pregnancy was progressing, how the wedding plans were coming along, and whether or not Elizabeth had bought a car. Now that Aunt Sally and Uncle Milt's daughter, Carol, is grown and has an apartment of her own, I guess Aunt Sally needs someone else to nurture.

"We're going to hit the used car lots with Elizabeth this weekend," I said. "Pamela is in her sixth month, and Patrick and I have to buy furniture."

"Is there an end to this unit, Alice?" she asked. "I mean, how far, exactly, does this Mr. Everett carry things?"

"Well, Pamela's not going to actually deliver in class, if that's what you mean," I said.

"And how have your father and Miss Summers been getting along?" If there's any trouble afoot within seven hundred miles, Aunt Sally can smell it.

"I don't know. I don't ask," I said.

"Well, I suppose that's best. You never really know what's going on in a relationship anyway, do you? Before your mother met Ben, we were sure she was going to marry someone else," Aunt Sally told me.

"She was?" I said, surprised.

"You never heard of Charlie Snow?"

It rang a faint bell. Somewhere, sometime, I seem to remember someone saying to my dad, "Better watch it, or I'll run off with Charlie Snow." I hadn't heard that line for years. I guess I'd always thought of Charlie Snow as a mythical creature, sort of like the bogeyman.

"That was her boyfriend?" I asked.

"Yes. And I think he was on the verge of proposing when Marie met Ben. Your dad absolutely swept Marie off her feet. I never would have guessed it in a million years."

"What was he like—Charlie Snow?"

"Well," said Aunt Sally, "he was as tall as Marie, lots of muscles, I remember that. He used to whirl her around as though she were some petite thing. A little too fast-talking for my taste. He had money, certainly more than Ben. I think he had a degree in business or something. Went to work for IBM."

"And?"

"And along comes Ben, an inch or so shorter than Marie, not exactly muscular, not much money, quiet as Charlie was loud, and your mom fell in a big way. To tell you the truth,

I think it was Ben's love letters that did it. As far as I know, Charlie Snow never wrote her any letters, but she'd get one from Ben and her eyes would fill with tears, he was that romantic. She set her heart on Ben McKinley and never looked back. And I'm glad she didn't."

I tried to imagine my mom in the arms of a muscular man named Charlie Snow who whirled her around. In the end, she'd chosen Dad. Maybe there was hope for him yet.

"Dad," I said at dinner. "This is a personal question."

"About my life or yours?" he asked.

"Yours."

"Watch it, Al."

"All you have to say is yes, no, or no comment."

"Now, Al . . ."

"Have you and Miss Summers ever—?"

"Alice!"

". . . corresponded," I finished. "Ha! Gotcha!"

"Corresponded?"

"Have you ever sent her any letters?"

"I may have, a note or two. Why? Have they turned up in the *Washington Post*?"

"No, I just think . . . women love to get letters, that's all."

"Thank you, Alice, for your very deep concern about my love life. I shall certainly take your suggestions under advisement," he said, which was another way of telling me to bug off.

· · ·

It was a week later, on Sunday afternoon, that Pamela, wearing her pillow again, Elizabeth, and I made the rounds of used car lots looking for a car for Elizabeth. We had dressed as sophisticated as we could so the salesmen would think we were eligible, and with Pamela's abdomen as evidence, I guess the salesman thought we were bona fide customers.

"I'd like to see something in a good used car," Elizabeth said. She was wearing hose and heels and had piled her dark hair up on top of her head with a comb. She could have passed for eighteen.

The salesman was all smiles. "Certainly. For you?"

"Yes. I asked my friends to help me pick it out."

The salesman's eyes settled on Pamela and me, but especially Pamela. Especially her abdomen. He smiled at us, too, but I could see he would have preferred we weren't there. Were we going to make or break a deal? he probably wondered.

"Why don't you tell me the kind of car you have in mind, and the price range, and then we'll find one custom-made just for you," he said.

"Let's start with the car first and then talk price," Elizabeth said. She had obviously been coached by her father. "I want a safe car, low maintenance, one that will give me several years of trouble-free service before it needs any major work."

The salesman jotted it down, or pretended to. Actually, when I stole a look at his worksheet later, he had drawn three happy faces, probably an indication he was dealing with three airheads whom he could sweet-talk into anything.

"And what about special features?" he asked. "Besides safety and durability, what would you most like to have in your car?"

"A stereo," said Elizabeth.

The salesman smiled politely.

"Leather upholstery," said Pamela, without thinking, and I had to nudge her to remember that Elizabeth was doing the choosing.

"Anti-lock brakes," Elizabeth went on, reading off the list her father had made for her. "Dual air bags, power steering, power brakes, air-conditioning—"

"The works, in other words."

"And a holder to set my Coke in," Elizabeth finished, wanting to add a little something of her own.

The salesman gave a polite cough to stifle a laugh. "Are we talking, uh, Mercedes here?"

"Oh, no, I could never afford a Mercedes," Elizabeth said quickly.

"A Lincoln Town Car?"

"Probably not."

"Well, that narrows it down some. I don't have anything

on the lot at this moment with dual air bags, but I would suggest you look at this Buick Century over here," the salesman said.

It was sky blue with dark upholstery. I could see Elizabeth's eyes light up as soon as she saw it. The salesman showed us all the features, but they meant nothing much to me. The only thing I understood was the rear window defroster.

We looked at four more cars, and finally Elizabeth asked to see the Buick again.

Now the salesman was eager. He was closing in for the kill.

"I'll give you the key and you can road test it yourself," he said.

We stared at him in horror. Naturally, none of us had a license yet, least of all Elizabeth, who is the youngest.

"No, no," she said. "We'll sit in the backseat and you drive it for us."

The salesman looked puzzled.

"You can tell a lot about how a car rides by sitting in back," said Pamela.

So the three of us climbed in the backseat, and the salesman took us a couple of miles down the road, explaining the features all over again.

"It certainly is smooth back here," I said.

"Yes, I thought maybe I was having labor pains a few minutes ago, but now they seem to have stopped in this wonderful car," said Pamela.

The salesman studied us uncertainly in the rearview mirror.

At a traffic light, we looked over and saw Brian in the car next to us, sitting beside his father.

Pamela rolled down the window and we all screeched and waved.

Brian turned, stared, then rolled down his window.

"Hey, what's up?" he called, looking at the salesman in the front seat.

I don't know what got into Pamela. "We're being abducted!" she shouted. "Call the police!"

"Pamela!" I gasped.

"What?" said Brian, looking at the salesman again.

"Now just a minute," said the salesman.

"Get the license number!" called Pamela as the light changed and the Buick bolted forward.

"What the heck—?" the salesman said, and turned at the next corner. Brian's father cut across a lane of traffic and turned, too.

"Pamela!" Elizabeth kept saying under her breath.

Brian's father pulled right up beside us, forcing the Buick to stop. Brian got out.

Brian's father got out, too. "You girls all right?" he asked, coming over.

Elizabeth flattened herself against the back of the seat, while Pamela sat with one hand over her mouth, her body heaving in silent laughter.

"I don't consider this very funny," the salesman said. "Maybe your time isn't valuable, girls, but this is my job."

"We're really sorry, but she's been this way ever since she got pregnant. I think it's a sort of psychosis," I said.

Brian's father stooped down and stared at Pamela.

"*Who's* pregnant?"

"Dad, let me explain," said Brian. "It's an assignment."

"We're going back," said the salesman, and pulled out into the road again.

Pamela waved gaily at Brian and his father as the Buick moved away, and as we stared out the rear window, Brian was talking earnestly to his father there in the street.

I think the salesman would cheerfully have dumped us all in a gravel pit.

We trooped into the sales office, though, and Elizabeth asked him to make the very best offer he could.

"I could only pay a little bit a month," she told him. "Show me the smallest amount I could pay to buy the car."

The salesman took his calculator and for the next five minutes, worked at the figures. "The best deal I can give you is two hundred dollars a month," he said. "This beauty has only thirty-six thousand miles on her. Mint condition. I could let you ride it out of here today for eighty-nine hundred dollars."

"Two hundred a month for how many months?" I asked.

"You'd have it all paid for in six years. Six years, and the car is yours."

I've never been real good in math, but I took my notebook and scribbled a little. Two hundred dollars a month is

$2,400 a year, times six is $14,400, close to twice the so-called selling price.

I showed the figures to Elizabeth.

"Well, thanks a lot, but I'll have to talk it over with my dad," she said.

The salesman looked disgusted. "Hey, that car isn't going to stay on this lot more than one weekend. I can hold it till tomorrow, maybe, but after that it's God's gift to the first customer who puts up the down payment."

"I can't do anything without Daddy's permission," said Elizabeth staunchly.

"Well, let's just go over that deal again and see if we can't do a little better."

I could see the panic in Elizabeth's eyes. What if the salesman made her an offer she couldn't refuse?

"I'm having pains," Pamela said suddenly.

The salesman looked around.

"She's having pains," I said.

"Do you think we should call an ambulance?" asked Elizabeth.

"No, just get me back to the bus stop, and I'll be fine," Pamela told us.

The salesman watched us go, slowly shaking his head.

In Mr. Everett's class on Monday, Karen gave her report on shoplifting. She had obviously done a lot of research and interviewed some police officers.

With a lot of giggling from us, she stood in front of the class and told how it all happened—hypothetically, of course: "Well, at first it was just a dare from my friends," she said. "It was a tube of Revlon lipstick from the mall, and I really couldn't believe how easy it was. There was nobody in that aisle, and I just picked it up, tucked it in the palm of my hand, and a couple of minutes later, dropped it in my jacket pocket. I paid for a magazine at the checkout counter and walked out with a lipstick, too.

"Then it was sort of a game. I took things I didn't even want or need just to see if I could do it. There was a kind of thrill, like I was getting away with something. And the next time I'd want to go for something bigger."

Even though we all knew that Karen's report was imaginary, it came across as real, and by the time she was halfway through, all the giggling had stopped.

"It was the feeling that if they didn't care any more than to leave their stuff around where anyone could walk off with it, they deserved to have it stolen. Like I was teaching them a lesson. Doing them a favor, even! So at first it was a game, then it became a habit, and finally, if I went to the mall and didn't lift something, I felt incomplete. Once I even went back just to shoplift something I didn't get the first time."

Nobody made a sound, and Karen continued: "Then one day I lifted a watch. I was standing at the counter looking at jewelry, and when the clerk looked away for a moment, I just slipped the watch in my purse. I moved slowly away, from counter to counter, and finally stepped out the door. I was real surprised when a man took me by the arm and said, 'Security officer, Miss. I'll have to ask you to come to the office, please.' Part of me was saying, 'This can't be happening,' and the other part was saying to the man, 'What took you so long?' "

Karen went on to tell about the shoplifting charges on her record, and how she was fired from her part-time job when her boss found out about it.

"Excellent job!" said Mr. Everett. "You covered all bases, Karen. That's what I want to see, class, a lot of 'what ifs.' These can help you imagine the future."

We talked some more about what charges on your record could mean, and then Mr. Everett turned to Jill, just as the session was ending: "Jill, how is your assignment coming? Haven't heard from you for a while."

"It's not," Jill said sullenly.

"Why is that?"

"I told you, Mr. Everett. It stinks! It's so *boring!*"

The smile on Mr. Everett's face disappeared. Usually he's genial and soft spoken, but this time all the humor was gone.

"Your assignment is due next week," he said. "And I expect you to have it done. As I explained before, we don't always get a choice as to things that happen to us, but we can choose what we do about them."

"I want another assignment," Jill said. "I'll do *any*thing but this one."

"It's the only assignment you'll get," Mr. Everett said, "and I expect it on my desk a week from today."

Most of the girls had stopped hanging around Mr. Everett as much as they had the first weeks of school, because it was obvious he had a lot more between the ears than his Robert Redford looks, not to mention the wedding band on his finger.

The incident with Jill only made Elizabeth like him more. He was strong, he was fair, he was gentle, he was firm, and he was hers—her teacher, anyway. I even began to wonder if you *could* love a person with your eyes alone. Elizabeth certainly made it seem easy.

$\mathscr{I}$NTO THE LION'S DEN

$\mathscr{P}$atrick and I shopped for furniture after school. We chose the cheapest store we could find. We were learning.

It felt really, really weird to be walking through a department store talking about mattresses and stuff.

"King-sized, definitely," said Patrick. "My folks have a king-sized bed. When I was little, I used to crawl in with them in the mornings and they didn't even know I was there."

I tried to imagine Patrick in his pajamas at age three.

"What are you smiling about?" he asked me, and flicked my arm.

"You in your jammies," I said. "I'll bet they were Bambi jammies, with little pictures of Bambi all over them."

"Nope," he said. "Pirates. Though I did have one pair of Winnie the Pooh." We laughed.

"What kind of furniture do you like, Patrick?"

"Chrome and glass. Heavy looking. Modern. What about you?"

"The only thing I ever really wanted was a four-poster bed."

"Oh, no! Not that! I'd always be banging my feet on the end board."

"Well, you choose the bed then. But I want a big dining room table. I like to think of my dining room after I'm married as full of people, all laughing and talking."

Patrick glanced over at me. "Kids?"

"Well, some of them, maybe. Relatives, I guess."

We were sauntering along, eating a sack of bridge mix that Patrick had bought, and he had one arm around me. I began to wonder if Mr. Everett knew what he was doing when he assigned us to be married. Then I remembered he had handpicked the assignments for the class after he'd known us for a week, and he'd probably figured that Patrick and I could handle it. It felt good to think that the teacher trusted us.

"How many children do you want?" I heard Patrick saying.

"We have to decide that, too? Right now?"

"No, I'm just curious."

I thought about it. "How about two boys and two girls?"

"Could end up with four girls or four boys, you know."

"That wouldn't be so awful."

"I'd say no more than two. You really shouldn't, you know, because of the population explosion."

"Four is an explosion?"

"Figure it out. Start with the two of us: We have four kids, each of them has four kids, each of them has four kids. If we lived long enough to see our great-grandchildren, we would have produced sixty-four people in just our lifetime."

"So?"

"So if everybody had four kids, where would you get the water for all those people? And food and oil? And what do you do with all the stuff they throw away?"

We were definitely going for an A+ on our report. Patrick had thought of everything.

We stopped to look at a bedroom set. "How much do we have left to spend on furniture?" I asked.

Patrick looked at our figures on the assignment sheet.

"Five hundred dollars," he said. "That's it."

I sucked in my breath.

It was hard to explain to the salesman about the assignment. First of all, he didn't believe us. I think he thought we were really getting married and trying to pretend we weren't.

"I don't know," Patrick said as he looked over the bedroom sets. "That mattress looks pretty flimsy to me."

"Try it!" the salesman said. "The only way to try a mattress is to lie down on it."

So Patrick stretched out on the bed.

"You've got to sleep there, too, little lady, so you'd better try it, too," the salesman said, winking at Patrick.

"Come on," said Patrick.

People were starting to look our way, and I knew Patrick

would just keep coaxing me, so I lay down on the mattress, too, about three feet away from Patrick. Would we be doing this someday for real? I wondered. Lying down on a mattress in a furniture store while people looked at us and smiled? I stayed about three seconds and got up.

"It's okay," I said. The cheapest mattress and box springs we could find was $267. That left $233 for everything else.

We looked at couches, but the one Patrick liked was $1,250. So for our $500 we ended up with a double-bed mattress and springs, a dinette table and four chairs, and a small chest of drawers. That was it. The salesman must have felt sorry for us because he said he'd throw in a bed frame and a lamp. I think he was really surprised when we thanked him but turned it down.

"You know," Patrick said as we headed home, "if we had to start out with the kind of wedding we've planned, a budget honeymoon to Niagara Falls, and furniture like this, I'd feel dirt-poor."

"We *are* dirt-poor, Patrick! I've got about thirty dollars to my name. What do you have?"

"Well, more than that."

We finished the bridge mix.

I could see exactly what Mr. Everett was getting at in his assignments. It wasn't just the money involved, it was setting priorities, figuring out what was really important and what wasn't.

"Dad, before you and Mom married, did you save money to buy furniture?"

"We married on a shoestring," he told me. "On absolutely nothing. I was still in graduate school and all I had was two hundred dollars in the bank. That was it. Your mom got a job at three dollars an hour, and we waited until we had saved two months' rent. Then we married."

"What did you do for a wedding?"

"I think we gave both the organist and the preacher a twenty-dollar bill. Your mom did buy a dress, though. That was important to her."

"What about flowers?"

"Your aunt Sally got them from the neighbors."

"Cake?"

"Your grandmother baked it."

"Photographer?"

"One of your uncles. Just snapshots, that's all."

"Furniture?"

"We spent a hundred dollars at a second-hand store."

I realized then that Patrick and I no more understood "dirt-poor" than we understood atomic physics. Mr. Everett knew his stuff.

That may have been true, but when I got to school on Thursday, Mr. Everett, wasn't there. We had a substitute teacher named Miss Larson, who said she would probably be finishing out the unit with us.

"Why?" asked Mark Stedmeister. "Is Mr. Everett sick?"

"No, he's not sick," said Miss Larson.

"Did something happen in his family?" asked Pamela.

"Class, all I'm told when they call me is that I'm filling in for a teacher, so you'll have to direct your questions elsewhere. Now . . ." She had the lesson plan book in front of her. "I see that four of you have completed your, uh, rather unusual assignments, and the rest of you have a way to go. Alice and Patrick, how are you coming with yours?"

We gave our report on buying furniture.

When the bell rang, everyone was talking about Mr. Everett. Elizabeth seemed devastated.

"What do you suppose happened?" she kept saying anxiously.

"Maybe there was an emergency in his family and he'll be back in a few weeks," I suggested.

"I bet he won't," said Jill.

There was something about the way she said it.

"Why?" I asked.

"Not after what he did to me."

Pamela, Elizabeth, Karen, and I all stopped in the hallway.

"What are you talking about?" I asked.

"You think he's such a great teacher and all, but actually, he's a lech."

"He *isn't!*" said Elizabeth.

"Ha! You don't know him like *I* know him," said Jill, and started on down the hall, but we charged after her.

"What do you mean? Did you report him or something?" asked Pamela.

Jill pressed her lips together.

"*Did* you?" Karen probed. "Come on, Jill, if he did something, we ought to know about it."

"I felt I *had* to report it," said Jill. "I didn't ask for him to be suspended or anything. I figured he'd just get a warning."

"He's suspended?" Elizabeth looked sick.

"What did he *do?*" Pamela insisted.

"If you promise not to tell anyone," Jill said secretively.

"Jill, the whole school's going to hear about it if he's suspended. Tell us," said Karen.

"Well, I went up to his desk after class to ask him a question," Jill's eyes looked straight ahead, "and he . . . started talking about my body."

We were all staring. "You just asked him a question and he mentioned your body?" I said. "What was the *question?*"

"About our assignments, what else? I can't remember his exact words, but it was something like, 'You have the body of a woman and should start thinking about what women do,' or something. And then he put his arm around me."

We were all stunned. I heard Elizabeth swallow. "What did he mean, 'start thinking about what women do'?" she asked.

"Oh, Elizabeth, grow up," said Pamela. "What do you *suppose* he meant? What did you do, Jill?"

"I left the room, what else? Do you think I was going to stand there and let him paw me?"

"He seemed so nice," I said.

"I thought so, too," said Jill.

Elizabeth went into the rest room and cried.

I couldn't get it out of my mind. All during study hall, I tried to imagine Mr. Everett saying that to Jill, and suddenly I actually remembered it. I was there! I heard!

I sat with my hand over my mouth, trying to play the conversation back in my head. I had been at the reference table in the back of the room, and Jill had gone up to Mr. Everett to complain for the umpteenth time about having to bury her grandmother.

Look at me! Isn't that what she had said? And she'd motioned toward her breasts. Something about looking older than she really was and how this was going to . . . cause her a lot more problems than burying her grandmother.

What did *he* say? My head swam. *If you've got the body of a woman . . .* Yes, he did say that.

I didn't see Jill at lunch and kept my thoughts to myself, but in gym that afternoon I confronted her in the locker room.

"Jill, I was there in the room the day you say Mr. Everett made a pass at you. It wasn't like you said it was."

"It was!"

"You're changing it all around, and you know it."

"I am not! I know what I heard, Alice. But I wouldn't have told anyone if I'd known he was going to be suspended."

"Well, I know what I heard, too. And you shouldn't have

said anything at all, because nothing happened. You've got to go to Mr. Ormand and tell him."

"Are you crazy? It was hard enough going to him in the first place."

"Jill, you *have* to! How could you do this to Mr. Everett? Everyone *loved* him!"

"I don't have to do a thing. I simply reported what happened, and the rest is up to Mr. Ormand."

I missed my bus after school. I didn't tell anyone where I was going or what I was going to do. I went right to the office and asked to talk to Mr. Ormand.

"I'm not sure he's in," said the secretary. "Let me check."

"It's really important," I told her.

She disappeared down the little hallway where all the offices were, and suddenly she was back with Mr. Sorringer.

"Mr. Ormand has a principals' meeting this afternoon," he said. "Is there anything I can do?"

I didn't want to talk to Mr. Sorringer. I didn't want to see him, hear him, or even be in his presence.

"Will Mr. Ormand be here tomorrow?" I asked.

"Yes, but he has conferences all day," the secretary told me.

I imagined Mr. Everett at home, not knowing whether he was going to keep his job. Imagined a committee being formed that would hear his case and decide who was telling the truth, he or Jill. I took a deep breath and followed Mr. Sorringer back to his office.

I didn't know if he remembered me as the girl who stared

straight through him in the halls, the girl who never said
"Hi." He held open the door for me, then closed it after I
came in. There were two chairs, so I took one and he sat
down at his desk.

"I'm sure I should know your name, but—" he began.

"Alice," I said.

He lifted his eyebrows slightly, as though to say, "Alice
who?" but I didn't give him a chance.

"It's about Mr. Everett," I said.

This time he seemed to freeze. I suppose he was thinking,
Oh, no, not another one.

"I hear he was suspended," I said.

This time Mr. Sorringer folded his hands on his desk blot-
ter and put on his professional face. "Well, I see the rumor
mill is alive and functioning," he said, smiling slightly.

Why did I hate this man so? Because I imagined his arm
around Sylvia Summers. Imagined his lips pressed against
hers, or his fingers caressing her back. He was like a robber
to me, come from California to take her away from Dad, and
I just couldn't stand the thought of his having her.

I tried to focus on why I was there.

"Well, I think I know why he was suspended, if he was.
A girl in our class told us she reported him, and she told us
why. I realized I was in the room when all this was supposed to have taken place, and it wasn't like she said at all."

Now Mr. Sorringer was really interested.

I explained about our unit on Critical Choices, and how upset Jill was because she didn't get one of the "fun assignments," as she called them.

"Can you tell me where Mr. Everett was when Jill was talking to him?" Mr. Sorringer asked.

"He was standing behind his desk, gathering up papers. Jill was standing next to him, maybe two feet away, facing him."

"Go on."

"She said, 'Look at me!' And she sort of motioned toward her . . . her chest. She said she looked older than her age, and that she was going to be faced with a lot more problems than burying her grandmother."

Mr. Sorringer looked confused. "Burying her grandmother?"

"That was her assignment. To find out all she could about burials."

"Okay."

"And Mr. Everett said, 'Well, if you've got the body of a woman, then you have to start thinking like a woman, and facing the kinds of problems'—no, maybe he said, 'making the kinds of decisions . . . that women have to make.' Something like that."

Mr. Sorringer nodded quietly, a little frown on his face, his hands folded under his chin now.

"Would you . . . would you say he said this in any kind of a suggestive way . . . as though he were implying more?"

"No!" I said it so loudly I even surprised myself. "*She* was the one who . . . who brought the idea of her body into it, not him."

"All right. Then what?"

I tried to remember. "I guess that's when he hugged her."

"Then he *did* touch her?"

"Mr. Sorringer, it was just a quick hug. He'd turned to leave and she was still standing there pouting. So as he passed her, he gave her a quick hug, just an arm around her shoulder—he had papers in his other hand. And he said something like, 'Come on, now, Jill, you can do it,' and left the room."

"He left the room before she did?"

"Yes. It was a one-second, one-armed hug and he was out of there."

"I see." Mr. Sorringer kept bumping his chin against his hands, thinking. "I know these details seem silly to you, Alice, but were their bodies touching? Were they face-to-face when he put his arm around her?"

"They were armpit to shoulder, his armpit, her shoulder. You could hardly call it a hug. It was just a gesture to show her he had confidence that she could do the assignment. I saw the whole thing, and at the time it didn't even occur to me that she could read anything into it."

"Then why do you suppose she did?"

"Because she's angry at him. She'd been asking him to give her another assignment, but he wouldn't. He says that sometimes we can't choose the things that happen to us in life, so we can't choose our assignments, either. Last Monday he asked her how hers was coming, and she said she hadn't done anything. He was pretty stern, and told her she had a week to turn it in. I think that's when she must have decided to get back at him."

For a whole minute Mr. Sorringer sat thoughtfully in the chair. Craggy-looking face, large hands, lanky body. I wished he'd say something so I could leave. The more I studied his hands, the more I imagined them in Miss Summers's hair, or stroking her face, or sliding down her hips. There was nothing else wrong with him that I could see, and if it wasn't that he was in love with the same woman my dad was, I might have liked him. I swallowed.

"I very much appreciate your coming to me with this, Alice," he said. "I'm sure this was difficult for you, and this is a ticklish situation, as you can imagine. We may need you to repeat this to a committee if we can't resolve it any other way. Would you be willing to come back if necessary in the presence of Jill and Mr. Ormand?"

"Yes," I said, and got up to go.

"I don't think I got your last name." Mr. Sorringer took the pen out of his pocket.

"McKinley," I said, and bolted out of the room.

$\mathscr{W}$EDDING BELLS

$\mathscr{A}$t dinner, I told Dad what had happened. Only I didn't tell him it was Mr. Sorringer I'd been talking to.

"I'm glad you went to the principal about this, Al," Dad said.

"What I don't get is how a girl can simply waltz into the principal's office and make an accusation, and the teacher's put on leave," said Lester. "You look at some girls cross-eyed, and they think it's a pass."

"That's a serious charge, Les, and the school has to investigate, of course, but the teacher gets his pay meanwhile. If they kept it under wraps and let him stay in the classroom while a committee looked into it, and he molested someone else, the principal would be in trouble for not acting sooner," Dad said.

Since I'd had to walk home that afternoon and it was my night to cook, I was trying to pretend that the He-Man dinners were something I'd made myself. I'd dished the food out of their microwave containers and arranged it on dinner plates, but I guess no one would believe I had actually roasted a turkey, made the dressing, and cooked the sweet potatoes and green peas, along with a cherry compote.

"What was Mr. Ormand's reaction when you told him?" Dad asked.

I was hoping he wouldn't ask.

"Mr. Ormand was at a meeting so I had to tell it to the vice-principal."

"Oh." Dad took another bite and chewed for a moment. "Well, what was his reaction, then?"

"I think he was afraid I was coming to him with still another story about Mr. Everett. Then, when I told him what had really happened, he got interested."

More chewing. More swallowing.

"What's the vice-principal like?" Dad asked.

"Ugly," I said. "His face looks like it has dents in it. Big chin. Sort of rocky looking." I kept my eyes on my plate.

"I meant, more in terms of personality," Dad said. He knew. He knew about Mr. Sorringer and Sylvia. He'd probably never even met the man, and he was trying to get a reading on his competition.

What should I do? I wondered. If I told the truth and said he seemed nice, Dad might get discouraged and just give up. But if I made Mr. Sorringer seem too awful, Dad might not try hard enough to get Miss Summers back.

"Well, he's ugly, but not *too* ugly," I said. "He's nice in a sneaky sort of way. I mean, *snakes* are nice when you see them for the first time, but . . ."

"Snakes?" said Dad.

Lester was looking at me from across the table. I tried to read his eyes, but it wasn't working. I didn't know what to do.

"I don't know, he seems . . ." I dropped my eyes again. "Sort of oily. Not very, um, sincere." I was as bad as Jill. I wasn't describing Mr. Sorringer at all.

"You got all that from a ten-minute conversation?" Dad asked.

"Well, that's just the way he seemed to me. Some people might like him, and some people might think he's great and kind and everything, but I don't think he's handsome in the least."

I was running off at the mouth and couldn't stop myself. Lester kicked me under the table.

"Well, now that we know Sorringer's a snake in the grass, what's going to happen to Mr. Everett?" Lester said.

"I would imagine they'll confront Jill with what Alice reported, and if she's smart, she'll agree that she exaggerated a little, and let it go at that," Dad told us.

That's exactly what happened. I saw Jill going into the vice-principal's office the next morning, and on Monday, Mr. Everett was back in class. I found out later that Mr. Sorringer had phoned her parents, and they had a talk with Jill. Jill admitted she had been angry and probably exaggerated a little, and the whole thing was dropped. By this time, of course, the class knew what had happened, and when Mr. Everett walked through the door, we all cheered and clapped. He looked surprised. Jill looked out the window.

He never did mention why he was absent, and when Jill gave her preliminary report on burying her grandmother, he treated her just like anyone else:

"Here's what I want you to consider, class," he said. "If every person who ever lived claims a three-by-six plot of ground on this planet, what happens? What is it we truly want to express in a funeral service? What other alternatives are there besides burial and cremation? Yet how might burial be more comforting to a grieving family? I'd like to see a little more perspective here, Jill. Otherwise, your assignment is coming along fine."

In the cafeteria later, we compared notes on all that had happened to us—hypothetically, that is—in our Critical Choices unit. Each of us had a different story to tell in our assignments: Patrick and I had decided to marry no matter what; Pamela had decided to have the baby and give it up for adoption; Brian had to do one hundred hours of community service for his DWI offense and attend a drivers' seminar, so he had to give up the football team; Jill decided to give her grandmother's body to medical science; Mark had to pay four hundred dollars a month for the next eighteen years for child support because the girl he got pregnant wanted to keep her baby, which meant he had to give up college and work two jobs; Karen had to pay a three-hundred-dollar fine for shoplifting and was banned forever from Wheaton Plaza; and Elizabeth decided she couldn't afford a car and would wait until she had the cash to pay for a used one in full. Until then, she'd take the bus.

Some of the other kids had been assigned problems with drugs, having a leg amputated, an alcoholic father, a mentally ill relative. We began to wonder how we could ever face life without having taken Mr. Everett's class.

"I probably learned more in the last six weeks than I have in my whole eight years of school," said Elizabeth glowingly.

"You know what we ought to do?" said Patrick. "Friday's the last day of the unit. Why don't we throw a bash?"

"Yes!" said Karen. "Why don't we throw a wedding for you and Alice, and we could all come as guests! Pamela can come to school pregnant."

"But don't tell Mr. Everett!" Brian said. "Let's keep it a surprise."

I was going to be a bride. No matter what else happened to me the rest of eighth grade, on Friday morning, in health class, I was going to walk, dressed in lace, down the aisle with Pamela and Elizabeth as bridesmaids. Patrick would be waiting up by the teacher's desk with Mark Stedmeister as best man. Brian said he'd be justice of the peace, which was sort of symbolic, you know, because Mark and Brian were semi-friends again, and it was nice having the gang back together.

That evening, I went over to Pamela's, where she and

Elizabeth had put together everything they could find made of lace—curtains, tablecloths, shawls, a blouse, even some mosquito netting. Mrs. Jones had a box of pins and she stood me in front of their full-length mirror.

"Here comes the bride!" sang out Elizabeth as she wrapped a lace tablecloth around me like a sarong.

"What would you like, Alice? It's your dress, after all," Pamela's mother said, sitting back on her heels. She was a tiny woman with silky blond, shoulder-length hair. "Big puffy sleeves? Long sleeves? Full skirt? Tight-fitting?"

I wondered what my mom's gown had been like. I saw it once in a photo, but I couldn't remember it now.

"Maybe tight at the top and full at the bottom," I said. That was good for a start.

Mrs. Jones herself was wearing a red shirt and tight black jeans. What would I be like if I had a mother who wore red shirts and tight black jeans? I wondered. Would we go shopping together? Would she teach me how to buy clothes?

Elizabeth had brought the veil she wore for her First Communion, and said I could have some yellow and white mums from their garden for my bouquet.

"This is so weird," I murmured as the gown took shape. How many times had we said that since Mr. Everett came into our lives?

"It's like it's really happening," Elizabeth said in a hushed voice.

"When it *does* happen, can we be your bridesmaids?" asked Pamela.

"*If* it happens," I said.

"Make it a black and white wedding, with long, slinky dresses for us," breathed Pamela. "Those are so cool, and I look great in black."

Once, while everybody was busy pinning and stitching, I stood there looking at myself in the mirror and my eyes grew moist. It happened so quickly I didn't even know it till I saw them glistening back at me. I was thinking how, when the big day really came, if it *did* ever come, my mother wouldn't be a part of it. She couldn't help me choose the dress, couldn't help with the flowers or invitations, wouldn't be there smiling at me in the first row.

I reached up and wiped my eyes before anyone could notice, but I felt a big hole in my chest, an empty place that nothing could fill. Dad and Mom had fallen in love and scrimped and saved to marry. Dad had written her love letters, and Mom had given up Charlie Snow. They'd made their plans, and look what happened. Mom only lived long enough to see me start kindergarten.

Was it worth it, all these bold and beautiful plans? Or did it just set you up for disappointment somewhere down the line?

Friday, just before health class, the three of us ducked into the rest room and I hurriedly put on my lace gown.

Elizabeth fixed the veil on my head, and put on a frilly yellow dress she'd worn for a cousin's wedding. Pamela, of course, was supposed to be pregnant, so she had on a yellow maternity top Mrs. Price had lent her.

The bell had rung five minutes ago, but a bride is always late, isn't she?

"How do I look?" I said, my heart pounding. This was crazy.

"Wonderful!" said Elizabeth. "Take your bouquet, Alice. Let's go."

Down the hall we went, and straight ahead, coming right toward me, was Sylvia Summers.

She stopped dead still, her eyes wide. "W . . . why, Alice!"
I giggled.

"Meet the future Mrs. Patrick Long," said Pamela.

"On her way to the altar," said Elizabeth, "only we're running late."

Then we laughed and told her about the assignment.

"Well, you look absolutely lovely, Alice, and if I didn't have a class this period, I'd come sit on the bride's side of the church," she said.

I beamed.

As we neared Mr. Everett's room, I could hear him saying, "Hey, what *is* this? Come on, guys, settle down now. We've got work to do here."

Somebody saw me through the doorway, gave a signal to the others, and suddenly everybody stood up and started singing, "Here Comes the Bride." I could feel my face flush. The blushing bride.

Elizabeth and Pamela went ahead of me, walking in measured steps down the aisle right in front of Mr. Everett's desk, Pamela with her protruding abdomen, and then I came in.

Mr. Everett stared, positively stared, with his mouth open. Then I saw his shoulders drop, and he grinned. Several of the kids had cameras, and flashbulbs were going off all over the place.

Patrick was standing up front with Mark, and Brian had on a black choir robe and was holding the dictionary as though it were a Bible.

I noticed that Patrick had a little carnation stuck in the lapel of his jacket. He was smiling at me. Was this nuts or what? I moved up toward him, laughing a little, and took his arm, and we faced Brian.

"Dearly beloved," said Brian, "we are gathered here because these two nutcakes, who haven't a penny to their names, think they can live on love and are about to go into debt over their heads. I now pronounce you husband and wife, and Patrick, you may kiss the bride."

And suddenly Patrick grabbed me in his arms and dipped me way back like people do sometimes on the dance floor. He kissed me so long, I almost stopped breathing. Everyone was clapping and cheering, and I figured if Mr. Ormand heard the commotion and walked in right now, Mr. Everett really *might* get suspended.

But when I got up, the pins on my dress gave way, and suddenly there I was, standing in my blouse and slip, the skirt in a heap on the floor.

It was too funny for me to be embarrassed for long. The guys all cheered as Patrick reached down and picked it up, and Elizabeth came to the rescue with a safety pin. Then Karen passed out the cake she had supposedly "lifted" from the supermarket, and we all sat around eating, laughing at Mr. Everett, who was still in shock.

"You kids!" he said. "You kids!"

I wore my wedding gown through study period, and then we all traipsed across the street to McDonald's at lunchtime to celebrate. The clerks stared, thought it was real, and said our Cokes were on the house. And all the time Patrick guided me around, one hand under my arm. I wondered if I'd have as much fun at my real wedding.

I put on my regular clothes for afternoon classes, of course, but before the day was over somebody handed me a couple of Polaroid photos of Patrick and me at the "altar."

That evening I laid them on the kitchen table without a word, and Lester was the first to see them.

"Ho-ly mo-ley, what's this?" he said.

"Patrick and I got married," I told him.

Lester looked more closely at the photos, then grinned and looked at me in surprise. "And you're still here? Still taking up space in this house? Darn! I thought I was rid of you."

Dad stared at the photos a long time, though, and said, "If I didn't know better, I'd say this was Marie at eighteen. She gave me a picture of her when she was in her teens. You look lovely, Alice."

I didn't actually believe him, but I wanted him to keep talking forever.

11

SURPRISE ENDING

$\mathscr{I}$'ll admit I liked myself in lace. I never thought of myself as a lace person, probably because Dad and Lester buy most of my clothes, so I've always dressed more like a boy than a girl. Unisex, at best.

But as I sat in my room that evening finishing my algebra assignment, I kept one of those Polaroid photos in front of me, and every so often I'd pick it up and look at it closely.

I just looked completely different. More . . . well . . . if not womanish, female. Instead of my rather straight, pageboy haircut, Pamela had created a few curls peeping out from under the veil, and the lace made me look more delicate, like something precious and breakable.

And Patrick! I guess I didn't have many pictures of us standing side-by-side like that, but he was at least four inches taller than I was, and his shoulders were more broad than I remembered. Then I realized he had on his blue blazer with shoulder pads, so I suppose that accounted for some of it. But still, he was looking down at me and smiling as though he meant it. As though we really were going to be married.

I glanced at the clock. Nine twenty-five. If we had actually been married this morning, what would we be doing right now? Well, maybe we'd be dancing somewhere, but we'd be *thinking* about going to bed.

On your first night, do you take all of your clothes off in the bathroom? I wondered. After you take a bath, does the bride put her makeup back on? At what point do they turn out the light?

I could hear Lester moving around in his room, so I tapped on his door and opened it. He had books spread out around him on the bed, and was drinking a can of Coke.

"Lester, what do you know about wedding nights?" I asked.

He choked on the Coke, and leaned forward as it dribbled down his chin. Then he swung his legs off the bed, wiping his face. "Good grief, Al! Give me a break!"

"Who can I ask if I can't ask you?"

"Ask Dad."

"He's on the phone, and besides, he spent his wedding night in a tent."

"What's the difference? People do the same thing in a tent as in a hotel."

"Not the kind of things I need to know."

Lester raised his eyebrows. "What do you want to know?"

"Who uses the bathroom first?"

"What?" He was trying not to laugh, I could tell. "Whoever needs it the most, I'd say."

"Lester, I'm really serious about this. I know it sounds dumb to you, but when I'm married, I don't want to louse things up. When one person comes out of the bathroom, does he get into bed or just sit around waiting for the other one and they both get into bed at the same time or what?"

"What *is* this, the Rockettes? Do you think everything has to be synchronized? Two people who are just married do what seems most natural to them. I would think that on their wedding night, in fact, a couple might want to go into the bathroom together."

"What?" I was aghast. "In front of each other?"

"If there was a Jacuzzi, certainly. But even a bubble bath in a plain old tub might be nice. Or soaping each other up in the shower."

I didn't want to think about it. I don't even like showers. I always get the water too hot or too cold, and I usually get it in my eyes.

I tried to imagine me and my future husband—Patrick, maybe—standing naked in the shower with water getting in my eyes. I imagined dropping the soap and trying to pick it up with one foot, or stepping on the soap and falling down, or both of us trying to kiss each other while a stream of water went in my ear.

"Okay, tell me one more thing," I said miserably. "When do they turn out the lights?"

Lester shrugged and this time he couldn't help laughing. "Al, some people *never* turn out the lights. They keep them on."

I thought I was going to have a heart attack. "Even while—?"

"Some people like it that way."

"Lester, I am *never* getting married! Never, never, never, never, never!"

I sounded like Elizabeth, but I didn't care.

I rushed back to my room and plopped breathlessly down on my bed. It was all just too embarrassing and awkward and gross and ridiculous and . . .

I heard Dad come upstairs. "What's wrong with Al?" I heard him say.

"She's never getting married," Lester told him.

"Good," said Dad. "I'll have company in my old age, then." And he went on into his room.

I brushed my teeth and put on my pajamas. I heard Lester go to bed. Dad was moving about in his room, though, and I felt I still needed to talk to someone. Maybe I could ask him how he and Mom worked things out on their wedding night—before they went to bed, I mean. If they went to a hotel first or spent their first night in the tent. I liked the idea of the tent. A pitch-dark tent with no shower to worry about.

I got up and went out in the hall. Dad's door was half open and his light was still on. I was just about to knock and go in when I saw him standing by his closet, his back to me. There was something in his hands, a shirt, maybe. No, it was flowered. Pastel flowers. It looked like silk. A robe. And he had his face buried in it, like he was, well, drinking in the scent.

I couldn't move. I couldn't go backward or forward. It was Mom's robe. I don't know how I knew, but I knew. And after a long moment, I saw his shoulders rise, as though he were taking a deep breath, and then he slowly hung it on a hanger again and put it at one end of his closet.

I went back to my room and softly closed the door.

We wore sweaters a lot to school now. Some days were really warm and we'd perspire, but mostly the air was crisp in the mornings—you could see your breath sometimes— and then it would warm up during the day.

In Mr. Everett's class, we were getting ready for the next unit, Responsible Living; in English, we were reading plays; in gym, we were learning folk dances; in world studies, we were comparing pre-Columbian civilizations; in algebra, of course, we were just doing algebra; and in home economics, we were learning to use a sewing machine.

I probably had more homework than I've ever had in my life, and I knew that after my three hours at the Melody Inn the following Saturday, all I'd have to look forward to was at least three more hours of homework. Patrick and I were seeing a movie on Sunday, but the rest of Saturday had to be spent over books.

The one nice thing about Saturdays, though, was seeing Marilyn Rawley at the Melody Inn.

"Alice Green Eyes," she called me.

Dad and I couldn't believe how much she had changed the Gift Shoppe. It was the part of the store Dad paid the least attention to, but the difference between the Shoppe run by Marilyn and the Shoppe that had been run by Loretta was the difference, Dad said, between the music of George Frederick Handel and the Grateful Dead.

Janice Sherman was pleased, too. When Marilyn wasn't busy behind the counter, she could help out almost anywhere in the store, and because she played both folk and classical guitar, she was able to give Janice ideas on ordering guitar music.

"What are you and Lester going to do this weekend?" I asked her. I could ask Marilyn things like that.

"Oh, I don't know. I think there's an Octoberfest somewhere up in Pennsylvania. We thought we might drive up there. Want to come?"

"No, I'll be going to the movies with Patrick." I knew Lester would murder me if I said yes.

I dusted the shelves where the little bronze busts of composers sat.

"This is sort of an embarrassing question, so don't answer if you don't want to, but do you ever think about your wedding night?" I asked her.

"My *wedding* night?" she said, the skin crinkling about her eyes.

"I mean, well, do you ever wonder what will happen?"

"Alice, today most brides know exactly what is going to happen on their wedding nights. Sometimes they've been living with their boyfriends for a couple of years, and the wedding night is no big deal. Gone are the days when a woman had no idea what she was getting into."

"Not entirely," I said, thinking of Elizabeth.

"Really? What do you want to know?"

"Not me. One of my friends."

Marilyn smiled. "Of course."

"It's just that I can't imagine Elizabeth ever undressing in front of a man or taking a shower with him or, especially, going to bed with the lights on."

"Well, then, tell her she doesn't have to do any of that."

"She doesn't?"

"Of course not." Marilyn rearranged the silk scarves on the shelf, the scarves with the *Moonlight Sonata* printed on them. "There aren't any rule books, Alice."

I looked at Marilyn. "You've never been married, though."

"Trust me." She smiled. "If you try to plan too much, you can ruin it."

So who was right? Mr. Everett? Marilyn? Dad? Lester?

Sunday started out to be a beautiful day. Patrick and I went to a movie in the afternoon and I didn't even get embarrassed in the love scenes like I used to.

The first time I ever went to the movies with Patrick, the couple on the screen were having this long passionate kiss, and Patrick and I weren't even holding hands yet. Now that's embarrassing.

I remember how I'd closed my eyes, hoping that when I opened them, the couple would be done. They were still kissing.

I'd closed my eyes again, and when I opened them a second time, the couple was *still* kissing, and Patrick was staring at me. That was even more embarrassing.

But this time Patrick already had his arm around me, and when there was a long, drawn-out kiss on the screen, he just squeezed me a little tighter, and sometimes leaned over and kissed my cheek. It was nice.

Dad had gone over to Sylvia's house to help put on her storm windows, which was encouraging, and Lester and Marilyn had driven up to Pennsylvania for the Octoberfest. Les got home about eight.

"Did you and Marilyn have a good time?" I asked.

"Great. Good weather, good food, good music, good dancing—I *love* October!" he said, opening the refrigerator and standing there to see what would jump out at him. "Hey, did Crystal call, by chance?"

"No. Are you dating her again?"

"Well, I've been calling her home for the past month and she's never there."

"Do you miss her?"

"Oh, we'll go out again," Lester said, finding some cheese and reaching for the crackers.

126

"She returned all your stuff, Les! Why would she go out with you?"

"So? She hasn't left the country, has she? Give me two more weeks, and see if I'm not taking her out again."

What happened next only happens in the movies. Dad was still over at Sylvia's—I guess he must have stayed for dinner—and Lester had taken a plate of crackers into the living room with him. I was getting ready to ask Lester for help with my algebra, when we heard footsteps on the front porch. The doorbell rang and I answered it. It was Crystal.

"Crystal!" I said, glancing quickly at Les in the living room.

Lester gave me a little grin and nodded his head as if to say, *See? Told ya!*

"Come on in," I said. "Lester's here."

"I didn't come to see Lester, I came to see you," she said, and she was smiling.

"Me?" I was so surprised, I forgot all about inviting her to sit down, so she just walked over to a chair.

"Oh, hi, Les," she said, and turned to me. She had her back to Lester. Her eyes were all sparkly.

"I've got great news, and I wanted you to be one of the first to hear," she told me. "I'm getting married."

Lester paused with a cracker halfway to his mouth and stared.

"You are?" I said, and then I saw the ring, as sparkly as her eyes.

"Well, oh, Crystal, congratulations! Who is he?"

"A really nice guy in my choral group. I used to go to high school with him, but then his family moved away. Well, he came back six weeks ago, and I guess it's what you'd call a whirlwind courtship. The last couple of weeks, I just *knew*. So when he proposed . . ."

"It's wonderful, Crystal!" I said, happy because she was happy.

"When's the date?" asked Lester.

Crystal didn't even turn around, just answered as though I'd asked the question myself. "The day after Thanksgiving. And Alice, I want you to be one of my bridesmaids."

"Me?" I could hardly believe it. I was going to walk down the aisle in lace again? "Oh, Crystal! Of course I will!"

I acted more like a flower girl than a bridesmaid, because I promptly leaped up and hugged her.

"We'll go over the details later—the dress and every-thing—but I wanted to be sure you were going to be here at Thanksgiving. Peter, my fiancé, has a brother he wants to be in the wedding party, and he's about your age, Alice."

Even knowing I was being chosen for my age didn't make me any less excited. "I'll put it on the calendar and circle it in red," I said. I *did* have a life! I *did* have things to put on the calendar!

"Thanks, Alice. I know I can count on you," said Crystal, and stood up to go.

"Who's the lucky guy?" asked Les.

"Peter Carey."

"You're really sure about this now?" Lester got up and walked a few feet toward her.

"More sure than anything I've ever done in my life," said Crystal, and went out the door.

On Monday, I thought about Crystal's wedding plans when I suppose I should have been wondering how Lester was taking it. But he seemed to be doing fine with Marilyn, and Dad probably wouldn't have been putting up Sylvia's storm windows if he didn't think he had a chance with her, so I told myself for once I could stop worrying and relax awhile.

At school, I had a chance to say a little something to Miss Summers, and I took it.

She was at the water fountain between classes when I stopped for a drink, and she said, "Isn't it a gorgeous October day, Alice? I love it when I can feel frost in the air."

"Are you going to sing in the *Messiah* with us again?" I said, before I could think twice.

"I will if I'm invited," she told me.

"You're invited. This is your formal invitation," I said.

"Then of course I will." She laughed.

I told Dad at dinner.

"She did? She said she'd come?"

"She said she would if she was invited, and I told her she was."

Dad looked really pleased. For once in my life, I'd done something intelligent.

It's funny about plans. I think Mr. Everett's right—I *know* he's right—when he says you should think about things *before* they happen so you can make the best choices. Even though things you didn't expect can happen—awful things, sometimes—or things may go just the opposite of what you planned, it's still better than no plans at all.

Look what happened to Mr. Everett himself. He went to college to be a teacher and was the best teacher he knew how to be, and then Jill made that stupid accusation. There was no way of knowing she'd do something like that. But if he hadn't been such a good teacher, I probably would have believed Jill's side of the story. I probably wouldn't have gone to Mr. Sorringer, and the class wouldn't have welcomed Mr. Everett back the way they had when he showed up again on Monday.

Dad and Mom didn't know when they got married that she wasn't going to live long enough to see her kids grow up, but if they hadn't planned and saved and married, I wouldn't be here and neither would Lester. Wasn't it worth the risk?

Some things, though, as Marilyn says, like wedding nights, well, maybe you just let happen. Maybe there's also room for some completely unrehearsed joy.

I was brushing my teeth around seven, when Elizabeth called.

"A . . . Alice, come over!" she said.

"What is it?"

"Just *come!*"

I didn't even put on my jacket, just ran across the street. Elizabeth met me at the door and she was as white as a pillowcase.

"What's the matter?"

"It's Mom."

"What?"

"Alice, I'm here in the kitchen," came Mrs. Price's voice, and when I went in, she was standing by the table, one hand resting on it, the other holding her stomach, just the way Pamela had done. But there on the floor where she was standing was a large puddle with little flecks of white in it.

I didn't understand.

"My water broke," she said, "and Elizabeth needs moral support. I thought I'd better get to the hospital. I'm having mild pains."

I was still staring at the puddle. At the little white flecks. Were they part of the baby? Like egg white or something?

"Where's your dad?" I asked Elizabeth.

Mrs. Price answered for her. "Would you believe, he went to Hechingers to buy more mulch for the garden? I'm not due for another week. . . ."

"Can we call Hechingers?" I asked.

"I just did." She suddenly bent over and winced. "Oooh."

Elizabeth collapsed on a chair.

"He's not there." Mrs. Price was panting slightly. "Now

I'm wondering if he went to Frank's Nursery first to price the mulch before he went to Hechingers. I've got a call in for the doctor. Elizabeth, write a note to your father and tell him we're probably at Holy Cross, that my water broke."

Elizabeth was staring straight ahead. Then I knew why I was there. I got a piece of paper and pencil and wrote the note myself.

The phone rang. Elizabeth and I sat motionless while Mrs. Price told the doctor her symptoms. ". . . fine all day . . . just a little heavy, you know . . . pressing on my bladder. Then about ten minutes ago, the water broke and I had a contraction. Two, actually—seven minutes apart, maybe. . . ."

When I heard her mention taking a cab, I said, "We can drive you. You won't need a cab."

"A neighbor says they'll drive me," Mrs. Price told the doctor. "Yes, I'll meet you in the emergency room." She hung up.

"Elizabeth, please go upstairs and put my pink gown in my bag. Also my robe and slippers. . . ."

Elizabeth stood up like a robot and started upstairs.

"And Alice," Mrs. Price said, "if we could call your father . . ."

I dialed home, my heart beating double time, and Lester answered.

"Where's Dad?" I asked.

"He went to the drugstore, I think. No, maybe he said the bookstore, I'm not sure."

"Lester, Mrs. Price is having her baby and we need you to drive us to Holy Cross," I told him.

"*What?*"

"Her water broke and she's having labor pains. The doctor told her to come to the emergency room at Holy Cross. Can you bring the car over?"

"Where's her *husband?*"

"They can't find him."

"Al!"

I remembered how Lester had passed out when I had my ears pierced. Could we trust him to drive on the beltway?

"Don't worry," I said. "She has a long time to go yet, and all you have to do is drive the car."

Twenty seconds later there was a screech of tires as Lester turned the car around in the street.

We left the note for Mr. Price on the kitchen table. Elizabeth had her mother's overnight bag, and I had hold of Mrs. Price's arm. We helped her down the steps. It wasn't until we were in the car that I realized nobody had mopped up the floor. Mr. Price would come home and find a puddle with white flecks in it and a note saying his wife was at the hospital. Maybe he'd think she'd exploded!

I got in the front seat with Lester. He was gripping the wheel like he was in an auto race.

"Lester," I said, "the slower and gentler you drive, the more likely you'll beat the baby to the hospital."

"Oh . . . okay," Lester said, and took a deep breath. His

driving instructor back in high school would have been pleased. He turned every corner as though we had champagne glasses on board, and he only ran a red light once when Mrs. Price moaned. By the time we reached the emergency room, I could smell Lester's sweat, but we made it.

A nurse came out with a wheelchair, and I was tempted to tell Lester to get in it.

"I'm going to stay with Elizabeth," I told him. "You go home and tell Dad where I am."

"And please tell Fred I'm okay," Mrs. Price called after him.

I never saw my brother so glad to be rid of a woman as he was that night.

Now it was Elizabeth I was concerned about. She had barely said a word all evening. We sort of tagged along after the nurse and the doctor and Mrs. Price in the wheelchair. When we got up to the obstetrics floor, the nurse showed us the waiting room, and we went in and sat down together. It was then we discovered we were still holding the overnight bag.

"Her bag!" Elizabeth cried, leaping up. "I've got her gown! I've got her slippers!"

"Honey," said a middle-aged woman across the room, "your mother doesn't need a thing till tomorrow. She'll be just fine. I'm waiting for my daughter to have her baby, and she'll be fine, too. This is the happiest ward, you ever think of that? The one place in a hospital where you're waiting for something natural and good to happen."

That seemed to calm Elizabeth a lot.

We leaned back in our chairs, tucked the overnight bag under the seat, and watched the set of double doors. Behind those closed doors, I was thinking, a dozen women were probably having babies right then. Yet I didn't hear a single scream. Not even a moan. Of course, there could be five more doors between us and them, but everything was quieter than I expected it to be.

"I have to go to the bathroom," Elizabeth said.

"Are you okay?" I asked her.

"I don't know." We walked out in the hall and down to the women's room. "Every time I think about what's happening to Mom in there, I just . . . my legs feel like they're going to give out from under me."

"She's not as nervous as you are, Elizabeth, and she's the one having the baby," I said. "She already knows what it's like. If it was awful, don't you think she'd be terrified?"

"You're right," Elizabeth said, but she still looked pale. She went into a toilet, and when she came out, she said, "I just don't see how a whole baby can come out of a woman, Alice, without tearing her all up. That's the awful part."

I shrugged. "Well, her body stretches, Elizabeth."

"But how? Alice, we're talking *big*!"

"It just does! Body openings stretch." I got an idea. "Look! Look at my mouth." We were standing at the sink now, in front of the mirror. "I don't have a very big mouth, do I?"

"Not exactly," Elizabeth said, washing her hands.

"Okay, now watch." I opened my mouth as wide as it would go.

"See how big it gets?" I said. "It's *supposed* to stretch. It's elastic. It's *made* to stretch." I took my fingers and pulled at the corners of my mouth until my lips were stretched into thin little ribbons.

Elizabeth studied me for a moment. Then she put her fingers in the corners of *her* mouth and pulled, too. We both stood in front of the mirror with our mouths wide open, stretching our lips out as far as they would go.

One of the gray ladies came in, the volunteers who help out. She stared at us a minute, then smiled sweetly. "I was sent to look for two girls who are waiting for Mrs. Price," she said. "I'll bet those girls are you."

"Did she have her baby?" Elizabeth asked, whirling around.

"No, but Mr. Price is here and wants me to tell his daughter that he's in the labor room with his wife."

Waiting was hardest of all. We went back to the lounge and stared at all the magazines about babies and parenthood. We stared at the coffee pot, and the paper cups with pink and blue designs on them.

There were three men in the waiting area who all looked like expectant fathers to me, and the middle-aged woman who was there for her daughter. There was a younger man, too, probably still a teenager, who was waiting. I wondered if it was his wife or his girlfriend behind the double doors down the hall. He kept looking around as though he couldn't quite believe he was there, as though it were all a mistake, and he should have been out at a ballpark or something with the guys.

Elizabeth turned to me suddenly. "Were you planned?"

"What?"

"Did your parents want you—I mean, *expect* you—or were you an accident?"

It was the first time that anyone had referred to me as an accident, but I remember Dad telling me once that they had waited a long time for me.

"Planned, I think."

"Me, too. But my little brother's a happy surprise, Mom says."

"You already know he's a boy?"

"Mom told me tonight. She had a sonogram a few months ago. She and Dad had sort of been keeping it a secret."

"That's great, Elizabeth. Now you'll . . ."

"Don't say it," she said.

I grinned at her, trying to make her laugh.

". . . see what a . . ."

She clapped one hand over my mouth and giggled.

". . . boy looks like . . ."

"Alice!"

". . . naked," I finished.

I think we were there for three hours and fifteen minutes. I know how many people used the coffee machine. I counted the number of windows in the waiting area, the number of pictures on the walls, the number of nurses that went by in the hallway.

We looked through every magazine, split a sack of peanuts, ate a bag of potato chips, and had a Coke. The gray lady came by and gave us a bottle of nail polish, and we did each other's nails. We watched a show on TV, split a doughnut, took a quiz in a magazine ("Are You a Risk Taker?" Alice—borderline; Elizabeth—no).

I think I even dropped off once or twice, and woke up at one point to find Elizabeth leaning against me, her mouth open, snoring. I sat very still because I figured Elizabeth was going to need all the rest she could get. I wondered how many of the babies born in this hospital had changed lives around completely, for better or worse. How many dreams they'd begun and how many they'd ended. I was going to suggest to Mr. Everett that he assign someone to visit a maternity waiting room sometime for the unit on Critical Choices.

Just when I thought my shoulder was going numb completely and I could never get out of my chair again without Elizabeth falling over, a masked figure came through the double doors, his eyes smiling. It was Mr. Price.

I nudged Elizabeth. Her mouth snapped shut and she blinked.

The man was holding a baby. "Elizabeth," her father said, "meet Nathan Paul."

Elizabeth's eyes opened wide this time, and she slowly

rose to her feet. I got up, too, and stood on the other side of Mr. Price.

There was a tiny baby with black hair and puffy eyelids, a small pink tongue protruding just a little through the lips. He was making soft smacking sounds.

"Oh, Nathan!" Elizabeth said, gently stroking his forehead with one finger. "You little thing! I love you to pieces!"

I never saw Elizabeth look so loving—or grown up. Did this mean she was no longer interested in Mr. Everett? In troubadours? Did this mean she would give up the idea of being a nun and become a mother instead?

Mr. Price let Elizabeth hold Nathan for a couple of minutes and then he even put the baby in my arms. I looked down at the funny little creature who was making weird movements with his mouth, and thought of all the choices *he* had to make in *his* lifetime. It made me dizzy. But for now he was set on automatic and didn't have to decide a thing. His body did it for him.

"Enjoy it while you can, kiddo," I said, and gently handed him back to his dad.

Find out what's next for Alice
and her friends in

OUTRAGEOUSLY ALICE

About the third week of October, I decided it was turning out to be one of the weirdest months of my life. Not that there have been that many of them—Octobers, I mean. Thirteen, to be exact. But here's what had happened so far:

Lester, my twenty-one-year-old brother, who has been juggling two or more girlfriends for several years, just got word that one of his *main* girlfriends, Crystal, was engaged to be married at Thanksgiving. And I was to be a bridesmaid. Now that's weird.

And of course I was still holding my breath to see whether Miss Summers, my English teacher last year, would marry Dad or our vice principal, Mr. Sorringer, who's in love with her, too.

Then Elizabeth, my friend who lives across the street, got a baby brother. At last she found out what a boy looks like naked. Is *that* weird, or what?

And finally, the student council at our junior high voted to create a haunted house for Halloween in the school gym to raise money for our library. What the school was going to do, see, was charge a buck fifty apiece to scare little kids half out of their minds. Patrick, my boyfriend, who's vice president of the student council, asked if I wanted to help out.

Well, why not? I thought. October couldn't get any crazier than it was already.

I was wrong. It got even crazier. Crystal Harkins's maid of honor invited me to a bridal shower—a *lingerie* shower—and I'd never been to a shower before.

But you know what? All of these things—the engagement, the bridal shower, the baby brother, the haunted house—were happening to somebody else. I was just on the outside looking in. Not much that is really dramatic, outrageous, and wonderful has ever happened to *me*—something to remember forever and ever. If there was a prize for the girl with the most boring life, I thought, I'd win it, hands down.

Here's where I miss my mom. If Mom were alive, she could have told me how to keep from being ordinary. She'd know what you take to a bridal shower, too. But because she died when I was four, I have to ask Dad and Lester, who don't know diddly, all my questions, and if I'm really desperate, I call Aunt Sally in Chicago. This time I tried Dad and Lester first.

"I've been invited to a lingerie shower for Crystal," I said at dinner that night. "Any ideas about what I could get her?"

"A chastity belt," Lester mumbled.

"What?"

"He's joking, Al," said Dad. He and Lester call me Al.

Lester just glared down at his tuna and noodles. I guess he figured his girlfriends would go on waiting all their lives for him to make up his mind, and it was really a shock that one of them got engaged.

"What *is* a chastity belt?" I asked, curious.

"A metal device that some medieval men bought their wives when the men were going to be gone from their fiefdoms," said Dad. "Only the husbands had the key. It was to insure that their wives would be faithful while they were away. Now you know how ridiculous this conversation is getting to be."

I couldn't believe it. "You mean it fit around their . . . ?"

"Exactly," said Lester. "Now shut up."

"But how did they go to the bathroom?" I have to know things like that.

"With difficulty, I imagine," Dad said.

I looked from Dad to Lester. That was so unfair! "What about the *men?* Did *they* have to wear chastity belts while they were gone to make sure *they* weren't unfaithful?" I demanded.

Lester winced.

I was indignant. "What about a metal pipe that fitted over their . . . ?"

"Okay, okay! Just drop it, will you?" Lester snapped.

He's been pretty touchy these days. Ever since Crystal returned all the things he'd ever given her and told us she was getting married, he's been a real grouch.

I'm not sure why I was asked to be one of her bridesmaids, but I think it's because her fiancé's younger brother is going to be in the wedding party. He's seventeen, and Crystal needs someone young to walk back up the aisle

with him. Or maybe Crystal's still mad at Lester and is trying to rub it in. Whatever, I'm prepared to enjoy myself.

"I don't see how you can buy Crystal anything without
knowing her sizes," Dad said, trying to be helpful.

"Big," said Lester. "Big hips, big boobs—a narrow waist,
though."

"Do *you* want to buy it for me, Lester?" I asked.

He glared daggers at me. "What do *you* think?"

I went up to my room after dinner and tried to figure out
what would look nice on Crystal Harkins. If she were to
step out of the bathroom on her wedding night and present
herself to her new husband, what would look best on her?
She has short red hair in a feather cut, and I imagined her
in a sheer white nightgown with lace over her breasts so you
could see her nipples.

I took the invitation out of the envelope again to see if
they gave Crystal's sizes on the back. They didn't. But there
was a little card enclosed that said the shower was being
given jointly by Betsy Hall, Crystal's maid of honor, and
Fantasy Creations, which, it said, for eleven years has been
making the kind of lingerie "every woman dreams of possessing, but only a few will dare."

"Huh?" I said.

I went straight to the phone and dialed my cousin Carol
in Chicago. She's Aunt Sally's daughter, and I always try her
first. Carol's a couple years older than Lester and, having
been married once to a sailor, she knows everything there is
to know in the sex department. The phone rang eight times

at her place, though, and she didn't answer, so I had to call Aunt Sally.

"Is Carol there, by chance?" I asked when Uncle Milt answered.

"Why, Alice, sweetheart! How nice to hear from you!" he said. "No, she's on a business trip, but your aunt Sally's right here. Just a minute."

"Alice?" said Aunt Sally. "What's wrong?"

I come from one of those families where if you call long distance, they figure someone just died.

"Nothing! I just wanted to ask a question."

"Oh! Certainly!" said Aunt Sally, sounding relieved. She's Mom's older sister, who took care of us for a while after Mom died, before we moved to Maryland.

"I've been invited to a bridal shower, and I'm wondering what to buy."

"Not Pamela or Elizabeth!" Aunt Sally gasped. Pamela's my other best friend, and we'd all three gone by Amtrak to visit Aunt Sally last June.

"No. An old girlfriend of Lester's, actually. She's marrying someone else."

"Good for her!" said Aunt Sally, who thinks it's time Lester settled down himself. "Now what kind of shower is it to be? Kitchen? Linen?"

"Lingerie," I said. "The kind every woman dreams of possessing, but only a few will dare."

There was a soft noise at the other end of the line. I think Aunt Sally had just sat down.

"Pajamas," she said finally. "Alice, you can't go wrong with pajamas. If I were you, I'd buy a pretty pair of pink pajamas, and I promise she'll thank you."

Crystal would thank me, all right, but would she wear them? I thought not. So after I'd talked to Aunt Sally, I dialed the maid of honor herself, who told me that I wasn't supposed to buy anything in advance.

"Just come," Betsy said, "and you can order from the Fantasy Creations catalog when you get here. We'll have Crystal's sizes, and she'll choose the things she likes. You might like to buy something for yourself, too."

Now *that* was the weirdest idea of all, because I don't have much of a body yet. I suppose that will come. At least I hope so. But what I really want is a life, not a new bra. I want to do things. I want people to notice me.

Elizabeth Price is beautiful, she takes ballet and piano, and she has a little brother to take care of, even though his poop is yellow and Elizabeth says she'll never eat mustard again. Gorgeous Pamela Jones, my other best friend, is taking tap and gymnastics, and Patrick's on the track team, the debate team, the student council, and the school newspaper. He's also in the band. Me? I'm just not a joiner, I guess.

When Patrick came over later, we walked to our old elementary school and fooled around on the jungle gym. He chased me over and under the bars but never did tag me, and finally we sat on the swings, turning around and around until the chains wouldn't wind anymore, and then we'd let go and spin the other way.

Patrick was talking about how busy he was going to be this year, with track meets and all, and suddenly I said, "Patrick, is it possible to get through life without joining anything?"

"You mean . . . like a church or a political party?"

"A band, a chorus, a club, a group, Girl Scouts, Boy Scouts, Triple A, *any*thing?"

Patrick dug his feet in the ground to stop the swing. "I suppose, but why would you want to? You allergic to people?"

"No! I like people! I just don't want to end up being like everybody else. Like a . . . a piano key, that's all." I thought that was pretty original, but Patrick thought I was nuts.

"Well, I guess you can have a full and interesting life without joining anything, but what *do* you do for excitement, Alice? Besides me, of course." He grinned.

Suddenly it seemed like one of the most embarrassing questions I'd ever been asked.

"I guess I figured I was busy enough," I murmured.

"A college might not think so," said Patrick.

"What does college have to do with it?"

"You have to list all your hobbies and extracurricular activities on your application, Mom says. And if you don't *have* any, well . . ."

I don't know how Patrick could even stand to kiss me later. I was a zip, a zero, a zed, a zilch. If someone were to take my pulse, I'll bet I wouldn't have one.

I marched straight upstairs to Lester's room, where he

was working on his senior philosophy paper, and burst through the door. "I need a life!" I bellowed.

Lester jumped a foot. "Good grief, Al! *Knock* first! You want to see cardiac arrest?"

"Lester," I wailed. "I have no body, no personality, no hobbies! I've got to join something quick. What should it be?"

"The army," said Lester. "Now scram."

I went downstairs to talk to Dad, but he'd gone out for the evening, so I lay on my stomach on the sofa, turning the pages of our school newspaper there on the floor, looking at photos of girls who had bodies *and* lives—cheerleaders, basketball players, singers, skaters . . .

On the last page, along with the ads for Hamburger Hamlet, Pizza Hut, Putt-Putt Golf, and Cineplex Theaters, was a boxed announcement:

JOIN THE CROWD! JOIN THE FUN!

Students: It's still not too late to join a club. Get the most out of your junior high experience. Don't let another week slip by without signing up for something extra. These clubs need new members:

Debate Team	*Girls' Soccer*
French Club	*Science Club*
Camera Club	*Explorers' Club*

I checked numbers three and six, tore out the ad, and stuck it in my notebook.